LEFT

TO

LOATHE

(An Adele Sharp Mystery—Book Fourteen)

BLAKE PIERCE

Blake Pierce

Blake Pierce is the USA Today bestselling author of the RILEY PAGE mystery series, which includes seventeen books. Blake Pierce is also the author of the MACKENZIE WHITE mystery series, comprising fourteen books; of the AVERY BLACK mystery series, comprising six books; of the KERI LOCKE mystery series, comprising five books; of the MAKING OF RILEY PAIGE mystery series, comprising six books; of the KATE WISE mystery series, comprising seven books; of the CHLOE FINE psychological suspense mystery, comprising six books; of the JESSE HUNT psychological suspense thriller series, comprising twenty four books; of the AU PAIR psychological suspense thriller series, comprising three books; of the ZOE PRIME mystery series, comprising six books; of the ADELE SHARP mystery series, comprising fifteen books, of the EUROPEAN VOYAGE cozy mystery series, comprising four books; of the new LAURA FROST FBI suspense thriller, comprising nine books (and counting); of the new ELLA DARK FBI suspense thriller, comprising eleven books (and counting); of the A YEAR IN EUROPE cozy mystery series, comprising nine books, of the AVA GOLD mystery series, comprising six books (and counting); of the RACHEL GIFT mystery series, comprising six books (and counting); of the VALERIE LAW mystery series, comprising six books (and counting); of the PAIGE KING mystery series, comprising six books (and counting); and of the MAY MOORE mystery series, comprising three books (and counting).

An avid reader and lifelong fan of the mystery and thriller genres, Blake loves to hear from you, so please feel free to visit www.blakepierceauthor.com to learn more and stay in touch.

CITY OF VICE (Book #6)

A YEAR IN EUROPE
A MURDER IN PARIS (Book #1)
DEATH IN FLORENCE (Book #2)
VENGEANCE IN VIENNA (Book #3)
A FATALITY IN SPAIN (Book #4)

ELLA DARK FBI SUSPENSE THRILLER
GIRL, ALONE (Book #1)
GIRL, TAKEN (Book #2)
GIRL, HUNTED (Book #3)
GIRL, SILENCED (Book #4)
GIRL, VANISHED (Book 5)
GIRL ERASED (Book #6)
GIRL, FORSAKEN (Book #7)
GIRL, TRAPPED (Book #8)
GIRL, EXPENDABLE (Book #9)
GIRL, ESCAPED (Book #10)
GIRL, HIS (Book #11)

LAURA FROST FBI SUSPENSE THRILLER
ALREADY GONE (Book #1)
ALREADY SEEN (Book #2)
ALREADY TRAPPED (Book #3)
ALREADY MISSING (Book #4)
ALREADY DEAD (Book #5)
ALREADY TAKEN (Book #6)
ALREADY CHOSEN (Book #7)
ALREADY LOST (Book #8)
ALREADY HIS (Book #9)

EUROPEAN VOYAGE COZY MYSTERY SERIES
MURDER (AND BAKLAVA) (Book #1)
DEATH (AND APPLE STRUDEL) (Book #2)
CRIME (AND LAGER) (Book #3)
MISFORTUNE (AND GOUDA) (Book #4)
CALAMITY (AND A DANISH) (Book #5)
MAYHEM (AND HERRING) (Book #6)

ADELE SHARP MYSTERY SERIES

LEFT TO DIE (Book #1)
LEFT TO RUN (Book #2)
LEFT TO HIDE (Book #3)
LEFT TO KILL (Book #4)
LEFT TO MURDER (Book #5)
LEFT TO ENVY (Book #6)
LEFT TO LAPSE (Book #7)
LEFT TO VANISH (Book #8)
LEFT TO HUNT (Book #9)
LEFT TO FEAR (Book #10)
LEFT TO PREY (Book #11)
LEFT TO LURE (Book #12)
LEFT TO CRAVE (Book #13)
LEFT TO LOATHE (Book #14)
LEFT TO HARM (Book #15)

THE AU PAIR SERIES
ALMOST GONE (Book#1)
ALMOST LOST (Book #2)
ALMOST DEAD (Book #3)

ZOE PRIME MYSTERY SERIES
FACE OF DEATH (Book#1)
FACE OF MURDER (Book #2)
FACE OF FEAR (Book #3)
FACE OF MADNESS (Book #4)
FACE OF FURY (Book #5)
FACE OF DARKNESS (Book #6)

A JESSIE HUNT PSYCHOLOGICAL SUSPENSE SERIES
THE PERFECT WIFE (Book #1)
THE PERFECT BLOCK (Book #2)
THE PERFECT HOUSE (Book #3)
THE PERFECT SMILE (Book #4)
THE PERFECT LIE (Book #5)
THE PERFECT LOOK (Book #6)
THE PERFECT AFFAIR (Book #7)
THE PERFECT ALIBI (Book #8)
THE PERFECT NEIGHBOR (Book #9)
THE PERFECT DISGUISE (Book #10)
THE PERFECT SECRET (Book #11)

ONCE GONE (Book #1)
ONCE TAKEN (Book #2)
ONCE CRAVED (Book #3)
ONCE LURED (Book #4)
ONCE HUNTED (Book #5)
ONCE PINED (Book #6)
ONCE FORSAKEN (Book #7)
ONCE COLD (Book #8)
ONCE STALKED (Book #9)
ONCE LOST (Book #10)
ONCE BURIED (Book #11)
ONCE BOUND (Book #12)
ONCE TRAPPED (Book #13)
ONCE DORMANT (Book #14)
ONCE SHUNNED (Book #15)
ONCE MISSED (Book #16)
ONCE CHOSEN (Book #17)

MACKENZIE WHITE MYSTERY SERIES
BEFORE HE KILLS (Book #1)
BEFORE HE SEES (Book #2)
BEFORE HE COVETS (Book #3)
BEFORE HE TAKES (Book #4)
BEFORE HE NEEDS (Book #5)
BEFORE HE FEELS (Book #6)
BEFORE HE SINS (Book #7)
BEFORE HE HUNTS (Book #8)
BEFORE HE PREYS (Book #9)
BEFORE HE LONGS (Book #10)
BEFORE HE LAPSES (Book #11)
BEFORE HE ENVIES (Book #12)
BEFORE HE STALKS (Book #13)
BEFORE HE HARMS (Book #14)

AVERY BLACK MYSTERY SERIES
CAUSE TO KILL (Book #1)
CAUSE TO RUN (Book #2)
CAUSE TO HIDE (Book #3)
CAUSE TO FEAR (Book #4)
CAUSE TO SAVE (Book #5)
CAUSE TO DREAD (Book #6)

CHAPTER ONE

She called herself Silver and she called herself French, yet neither of these things was true. She adjusted her lingerie top, pulling at the underwire and settling one of the bows. A gaudy, over-the-top display, but the clients seemed to like it.

She combed a strand of blonde hair behind one ear, standing outside the door in the dingy, red-lit hall. The faint scent of cinnamon candles lingered on the air, and the carpet pressed softly beneath her feet. Other doors, in dark alcoves, lined the hall, sealed from prying eyes. She heard the faintest tinkle of piano music playing over unseen speakers hidden in the ceiling trim. But the music couldn't completely disguise the sound of panting, of pleasure, and sometimes pain emanating from the rooms beyond.

Once she'd adjusted her outfit, Silver adopted a more docile posture. Her shoulders narrowed, her chest pronounced, her lip—ever so slightly—curled. She placed one foot just slightly behind the other, a leg cocked. The client sheet, which he'd filled out earlier, suggested the man wasn't into strong, domineering women.

And so she adopted a more bashful, hesitant demeanor, like a chameleon shedding its skin. Silver was an expert at providing whatever clients wanted.

In De Wallen, Amsterdam, her line of work was quite competitive. Over two hundred window brothels, with many more professionals operating in such establishments. People came from all around the world to taste and experience what Amsterdam offered.

She tapped tentatively on the door, even this gesture calculated. A soft, hesitant knock. "Hello?" she said, even adding the faintest quaver to her tone.

"Come in!" a voice called from within.

She opened the door, not too quick, not too slow, like a dancer flowing through the motions. She stepped into the room beyond, adopting a schoolgirl smile and a coy flutter of her eyelashes.

The man sitting on the bed resembled a supply teacher, or a dusty old librarian. He wore round spectacles and had early-onset worry lines creasing his forehead beneath a dark, but fading, fringe. He had pleasant features and kind eyes.

His hands were clasped in his lap where he sat on the bed. His shoes were still on, plus he was still dressed.

Peculiar, but not unusual. For first-time clients, it often took time to make them comfortable. Silver closed the door behind her with her bare heel, allowing her long leg to catch the man's eye with the entrancing motion available to all denizens of the gentler sex.

When the door clicked shut, though, leaving them in the comfortable room with its queen-sized bed and attached bathroom with a luxury shower, the man wasn't even looking at her.

Instead, his eyes were downcast, his hands still clasped in his lap like a priest at prayer. His cheeks were tinged red, and she watched his fingers tremble as he released his clenched hands and adjusted his spectacles. "You're very nice looking," he said in English, his voice shaking.

She had to hide a smile. She liked meek and reserved men. He wasn't bad looking either. Nice guys finished last, some said. In her experience, nice guys often finished first. She got paid the same either way.

"Do you think you'd like to get more comfortable?" she said, tugging at the strap of her bra to indicate what she meant.

The man shifted, raising a quizzical eyebrow beneath his fading fringe, but when he realized what she meant, he blushed suddenly, forcing a quick cough to hide his discomfort. "Oh—oh no, that's quite alright. Thank you. I'm—I'm okay staying dressed. Is that okay with you? Geez—sorry. I don't mean to cause trouble..."

He spoke English quite well but had a faint accent she couldn't place. She dropped a bit of her own docile posture. With clients like this, they were often just grateful to be in the room.

The window above the bed was covered in a faint, red gauze, allowing the fading evening light from the city beyond to bathe the room in a romantic, pink-red glow.

The scent of cinnamon from the hall also lingered in the room, and three tastefully placed blue candles sputtered in alcoves around the bed.

The man gave a wave of his hand, his fingers trembling. "I'm not here for... for *that*... I don't want what other men want."

"I see," she said, a purr to her voice. "You're a special sort of man, yes?"

He ducked his head again, smiling at where his hands were clasped once more. "You're special too," he said. "I knew it when I first saw you. You have very, very pretty hair."

Silver chuckled, a throaty, breathy sound. "You have kind eyes. You also have *me*. For the hour. What is it I can do for you, Mr..."

She trailed off, allowing him to provide whatever name he wanted to use. Instead, he just looked at her. "What do you think my name is?"

She paused. An unusual question, but her smile returned just as quickly. "I wouldn't know."

His left cheek dimpled. "What would you call me if you had to guess?"

She paused, a long finger against the underside of her own chin. "Hmm, let me see... I once had a puppy I loved. He had kind eyes too."

"What was his name?"

"Remus," she said. "I can call you Mr. Remus if you like."

"Perfect," he said, nodding. He looked up, meeting her gaze full on for the first time. His eyes crinkled in the corners; his premature worry lines softened as he looked at her. "And you're called Silver, yes?"

"Mhmm... I like you, Mr. Remus. So I think I have to inform you that if we go over the hour, you'll have to pay for another full session to continue this company. Which is quite enjoyable, I'll add. You are a great conversationalist."

He chuckled, his dark eyes twinkling. He waved a hand airily, relaxing a bit it seemed at the compliment. Silver hid a smile again. She liked this part, when the turtle crept from the shell. When her silver-tongue helped loosen the more uptight sorts. She was in the business of helping folks relax. It was one of the reasons she'd come here, to Amsterdam. She enjoyed her job, enjoyed this place. Particularly, she loved the people.

Sometimes, her clients could be creeps and weirdos. But the vetting process and the security team often helped keep such people at bay. Normally, her clients were the usual sort—bankers, lawyers, tourists, bus-drivers. People. Interesting people with their own lives and stories and secrets.

In this context, they often opened up, sharing things they wouldn't even whisper in their priest's ears. She liked the job. And tonight, it seemed, was going to be a good one. The man still had his clothes on and had made no overtures. Some of them just liked to talk. Of all the clients, this was her favorite type.

"Mr. Remus," she said, "do you mind if I sit next to you?"

His cheeks were still tinged red, but he didn't blush this time and, clearing his throat, he stuttered, "N-no, I mean, yes. Please. Here. Whatever you'd like."

Silver sidled over, not even bothering to sway in her usual way. She sat on the bed, next to her client, studying his silhouette. He was thin, wiry. Average height. Nothing particularly remarkable at all except those kind eyes of his, crinkled in the corners beneath the worry lines of a fifty-year-old on the face of a thirty-year-old.

"Silver," he said as she settled on the soft comforter. "Can I ask you something?"

"Yes, dear."

"Where are you from?"

He barely even murmured the question, eyes downcast once more.

"Ah, yes. France," she said instinctively. A lie. A soft lie, but one she often used.

He nodded slowly. Then, he switched languages. "Where in France?"

She blinked, caught off guard. "Umm, Paris, actually," she said.

It took her a second to realize her mistake. He'd asked her in Flemish—the man was from Belgium, then. She was also from Belgium, a lifetime ago. Or so it felt.

"I see," he said, his eyes more alert now, watching her. "Paris is nice."

She cleared her throat. "Y-yes. Yes. Enough about me, though. Tonight is about you. What do *you* want, hmm?" She leaned in, breathing softly in his ear, the warmth blossoming against his reddened cheek.

The man shot her a sidelong, shy glance. "I—well... If it's not too much trouble. There's a game I like to play."

She chuckled breathily. Here it was. They always opened up eventually. "What sort of game?" she purred.

"Do—do you mind if I show you, Silver? Please—if it's not too much bother?"

She grinned, leaning back suddenly, reclining on the bed, her blonde hair fanning out around her as she pressed to the pillow. "Show me, dear Remus. Just remember," she added, in a somewhat less sultry voice, "the contract and consent form you signed, yes. Anything outside the parameters listed there is expensive and requires express permission."

"Oh, no, no," he said wrinkling his nose in disgust. "Nothing like that." He studied her, staring at where she reclined, almost feline, on the bed, looking up at him. "I brought this..." He reached into his pocket.

She tensed, staring. Clients weren't allowed to bring their own toys. She relaxed, though, as he withdrew a silky, pale scarf, the color of snow. The scarf was perfectly clean and draped over his fingers. He rubbed the material tenderly, letting out a shuddering, shaking breath. He was illuminated in the red glow from the gauze over the window. She was stunned to see the faintest trickle of a tear crawling down the inside of his cheek as he sat there, perched on the edge of the bed.

He reached up with a shaking hand, holding the scarf, and wiped the tear away.

"Sorry," he sniffed. "Just... do you mind?" He extended the scarf towards her.

"I don't mind at all, Remus." She patted his arm and took the scarf with delicate fingers. "Like this?" she asked, lowering it slowly.

"Umm—no—no... just... Here, can I?"

She allowed him to gently bring the scarf up, wrapping it around her shoulders, adorning her like a queen.

She chuckled. "Normally men don't put more clothes on me."

He wasn't smiling anymore, though. His eyes had a distant, misty look to them. His cheeks were still reddened. He adjusted the scarf, like a photographer aligning a subject just so.

"Are you okay?" he whispered. "Are you alright?"

She nodded, shifting her shoulders a bit as he adjusted the scarf.

"Here," he said faintly. "Just let me—just a bit... Sorry, just a little here."

She rolled her shoulders, allowing him to raise the scarf a bit from her shoulders. The faint, gossamer fabric of sheer white drifted on the space between them like the tendril of some ghost. He wrapped the scarf a second time, and she waited patiently.

At least he was gentle about it. Some men could be downright brutal in the games they played. She'd been choked before. The scarf was a nice touch. She didn't mind—she was a professional anyway. Besides, she was almost... fond of this client. She'd never seen Mr. Remus before and she wasn't sure why he'd cared so much about calling out her lie of being French, but the tears in his eyes, his docile bearing, his meek posture. It was hard not to like the guy.

So she helped by arching her back and neck, giving him access as his trembling fingers fumbled with the scarf.

"Is there anything I can do—" she began to offer.

But then he tugged at the scarf. It tightened. She held her breath, conserving it. So he was a choker—she'd thought so. But it was always hard to tell until they actually started.

He tightened the scarf a bit more.

"Are you okay?" he whispered. "How are you feeling?"

She smiled at him, but didn't speak, conserving air. He'd already been briefed on the safe word. Been told the rules. Thirty seconds at a time. If she tapped his arm, he had to release.

She was fine, though. She'd made it as long as a minute in the past.

He tightened the scarf further, wrapping it around one hand and pulling. Now she couldn't draw breath. The air was chased from her throat.

She wriggled a bit, uncomfortable. Choking was fine, but not as fun as just talking. She would have sighed if she'd had the air to spare. Perhaps tonight wasn't going to be as fun as she thought.

He tightened the scarf further. Then a tear fell from his eyes. It splashed against her cheek. "I'm so, so sorry," he whispered. He leaned in, kissed her on the lips, gently. His lips were warm, and he smelled of aftershave.

And then he pulled the scarf sharply, yanking with both hands.

Silver's eyes bugged. Too hard. Too fast. She hadn't been prepared.

She tapped fervently against his wrist. But he just pulled harder, weeping now as he hunched over her like a gargoyle on the edge of a building. She tried to fight him, pushing at his chest, but he pulled the scarf tighter, tighter still.

He was still crying, still muttering an apology, but it was no good. She couldn't breathe. Help! She tried to scream, but it only cost her more air. She tapped his arm more feverishly. He ignored it. She tried to speak the safe word, but she couldn't speak at all.

She was choking. She couldn't draw air.

His grip was only tightening, his hands bunched around the edge of the scarf, yanking it up with all his strength.

Her face prickled, blood rushing, her arms tried to push him off, but he was surprisingly strong. Another tear splashed against her cheek, but it was no good, no use. Dark spots started pirouetting across her vision. She felt cold now. Exposed and so cold. So helpless. Nothing to do. No ability to scream. Couldn't move. Couldn't do anything.

Help! She thought desperately. *Please!* She tried to slap his forearm again, but the motion was weak, useless, pathetic.

He didn't care, either. What she'd taken for kind eyes stared down at her, full of tears as he choked the life from her perfectly sculpted body, both of them bathed in red light and the scent of cinnamon.

CHAPTER TWO

She was having second thoughts. Agent Adele Sharp didn't feel like an agent right now, standing outside Renee's place.

Night swept Paris, and Adele stood outside John's house on the edge of the city in a tree-sheltered subdivision. Pines prickled and rustled with the faint intrusions of whistling wind. Adele brushed her off-blonde hair back, her fingers grazing her sweat-prickled brow. The wind brushed her cheeks in a chill kiss, and despite her sweater she hugged her arms against herself, trembling.

But the chills weren't just from the wind, weren't just from the thin layer of the shirt beneath her sweater.

She felt like a child. A chastised kid, waiting for the inevitable punishment. Over the last couple of weeks, she'd struggled to keep her career, to hide the truth of what had happened in that garden with the man who'd killed her mother.

She could still see the stream of bubbles rising and popping on the surface of the flowing water. Could still see the way he'd kicked and struggled and then...

The way he'd died. She'd shot him twice. She'd made it impossible for him to push himself from the water. And then she'd stood back and watched him perish. She'd refused to render aid. Hell... she felt another prickle of chill wind. She had enjoyed watching him drown.

And then she'd lied. She'd told the DGSI that it had been a self-defense shooting. Had told them she'd been busy helping Claudia, Renee's daughter. She hadn't been able to save the monster.

Agent Sophie Paige suspected *something,* but the older agent seemed to have dislodged that bee from her bonnet. At least for now.

But the guilt was still eating at Adele's conscience. And so now here she sat, facing John's small home, scowling. His daughter lived with his ex, Bernadette. John Renee had recently increased his visiting hours, but he still lived alone.

At least their conversation would be a private one.

And yet Adele couldn't muster the courage to walk up to the patio and knock on the door. For nearly ten minutes now, she'd stood here, beneath the rustling pines, scowling at the house, fidgeting uncomfortably.

Maybe she should go for a run first, yeah... that'd help. A run would take her mind off it all. She'd always enjoyed running, especially in the morning. Sometimes, she'd put her earbuds in and just go for two hours.

But now, even the promise of exertion, of a body in motion, didn't hold the same solace as usual.

She just stayed there, planted like one of the trees, entirely motionless.

And then the porch light flicked on. Her heart leapt. A second later, a tall, muscular shadow appeared in the doorway. The shadow stepped onto the porch, taking the long, lanky, dark-haired form of John Renee. His hair, almost impossibly, was as immaculate as ever, even given the late hour. He had a single, superman curl that had escaped from his fringe, but the rest was combed back, slick with some type of gel.

A burn mark curled up his chest, along his neck and under his chin. Other than that, Renee was quite handsome. Adele had been taken with him for a while now.

He raised a calloused hand, fingers curling as he waved at her. He gave a faint nod, but then leaned back, his shoulder pressed to his doorway. He remained in the shadows, studying her.

Dammit. He wasn't going to make this easy, was he?

Adele had to bite back a surge of frustration. No... No, this wasn't John's fault. He'd been kind enough to agree to meet her. To speak with her. He'd been kind enough to stay up this late. She remembered the first time she'd ever spoken with John in private, one on one. He'd converted one of the abandoned, basement interrogation rooms at the DGSI into something of a bachelor pad, with his own distillery.

She could still remember the bitter taste of the homemade alcohol. Remembered the military pictures he kept on his wall.

Things had softened since then with John. Now, he spent time with his daughter. He was determined to be the sort of father he'd never had.

Adele missed the earlier days, when things had been easier. She missed simpler times. The wind picked up again, the tree above her hushing and shushing almost as if advising her to keep her lips sealed. Her body tensed, poised, but then she let out a faint sigh of resignation and broke into motion, moving up the sidewalk, eyes downcast, studying the cracks in the pavement illuminated by the streetlight above.

She reached the porch faster than she would've liked. She glanced up, wincing sheepishly. "Hey," she said.

John nodded back. "American Princess," he said in greeting.

"I've got something to tell you." Like ripping a band-aid, quick, fast, to the point.

John crossed his arms, his muscles pressed against his thin, nighttime t-shirt. He just nodded and made a wiggling motion with his hand as if to say *go on.*

But she couldn't. She didn't. The words wouldn't come. Her throat felt tight, parched, all of a sudden.

She let out a long, shaking sigh, but still wasn't sure where to start. Would John think of her differently? Would he like her less? Hell, would he hate her? Things had been going so well between them; she hated the idea of ending it all over her own stupid choices.

"Adele," John said suddenly, his eyes watching her like a hawk's. "You didn't cheat on me, did you?"

She blinked, then nearly laughed. "I—what? No!"

John let out a faint, shuddering sigh of relief. "Jesus—good. Shit. You had me scared there."

"John—it's serious."

He shrugged and tensed again. "You're not sick, are you?"

"Umm—no..."

"I see. Well. I'm fine playing twenty questions if you want. Or... you know, you could just *tell* me what's on your mind." His tone softened a bit, losing its usual acerbic edge. "You can tell me anything, Sharp. Truly." Then, quickly, he added, "As long as you haven't been sexting that asshole Leoni. You haven't, have you?"

She rolled her eyes now. He was only half-joking, but something about his humor helped loosen the lump in her throat.

"John," she said slowly, "I should have told you before. I... I should have..."

"This isn't about the painter, is it?'

She blinked, didn't reply.

"I see... Is it about watching him drown?" John raised an eyebrow.

Adele just stared at the DGSI agent, stunned. "I—I... *what*?"

John waved airily. "You shot him, disarmed him, then let him drown without helping, right? Failing to render aid, if I'm not mistaken."

Adele couldn't quite believe her ears. She also gritted her teeth in response to Renee's cavalier tone.

"John—you knew?"

"Wait—you're serious. This is about that?" He threw back his head and laughed. A single, humorless bark. "Adele, Claudia told me everything. I asked her what happened, and she gave me a play-by-play. I'm the one who told her to fix the story a bit for the cops. You think she thought to skip some of the details on her own?" He snorted, shaking his head. "Jesus, Adele—I mean, you look like you've swallowed glass."

"John, it's not funny. I killed a man! I watched him die."

"Sure. A monster. A serial killer." John shrugged again, picking at a fingernail now. He looked relieved, relaxed. A little bored.

Adele had been preparing for this conversation on the drive over, dread in her stomach. She'd tried to play out every eventuality. Tried to deal with images of John's look of severe disappointment. She'd wondered if he'd ever respect her again. But what she hadn't braced for, what she hadn't considered, was *this*.

Indifference. A bit of boredom.

Now he was yawning, barely hiding the gesture with a thick palm.

Adele could feel tears threatening her eyes. But she refused to cry now. Not in the face of this... Why was she even upset anyway? John wasn't mad; he'd known the entire time. He clearly hadn't cared.

"You're not mad at me?" she said, her voice trembling.

John looked up, suddenly stunned. He blinked and seemed to notice her expression for the first time. "Adele?" he said as if shocked. "Are you... you're not—oh, Adele!" he said, compassion in his tone, all of a sudden. He shoved off the door frame and took a single, giant stride to gather her in an embrace. His unshaven chin prickled against the side of her cheek. His breath was warm on her ear, competing with the chill of the wind. His body was firm, strong where he embraced her, holding her tight.

"Oh, Adele," he said, again, holding her.

She couldn't help herself. Something about the hug. About the sudden rush of concern to his voice. About the earlier indifference to the worst thing that she'd ever done... She broke down.

It was late. She was tired. It had been a long couple of weeks. Even as her shoulders shook and tears formed, Adele could feel her mind hastily reaching for excuses.

But it didn't change that she had her head pressed against John's chest, sobbing suddenly, ugly-crying. He didn't retreat, didn't recoil. They stood on his small, porch, illuminated by the naked bulb above, the trees rustling around them, the other homes in the subdivision all silent and dark this late at night.

"I—I'm so sorry," she sobbed, unsure who exactly she was speaking to. "I—I wanted to... I tried to—I just... Everything was so—I should've saved him. I should've helped!"

John held her tight, allowing her to cry, to speak. Once she'd calmed a bit, though, her face still buried against his chest, he murmured in her ear, "You did the right thing, Adele."

She shook her head furiously, her hair rustling where it swished against his t-shirt. "No—no I killed him. I could go to prison, John."

"That's not happening!" He said it in such a deep voice that his chest rumbled.

Adele sniffed, feeling embarrassed at the histrionics now, trying her best to gather herself.

"Adele," John murmured again, "You did the right thing. I hope you know that. You're not going to jail. You're not going to lose your job. No one else has to know. Over my dead body does anything happen to you over this. Get me? Over my cold corpse."

"How can you say that?" she whispered. The floorboards creaked as she shifted her weight from foot to foot. She pushed away from him now, still gripping his arm like a mooring rope, her cheeks stained, her eyes red. She imagined she looked awful. She stared at the handsome agent, shaking her head.

"The corpse part?"

"No—the... I didn't do the right thing."

John held up one hand, raising a finger as he numbered off, "You saved my daughter. You stopped a monster. You gave him every chance to comply. He died." He held the four fingers high and wiggled them. "Not a single thing you did was wrong."

"But—but I just watched him drown..." She swallowed, then, blurting it fast so she couldn't get cold feet and she said, "I enjoyed it! I wanted him to die! I liked it! John, I became the same thing as him. I... I'm a killer now. That's what he wanted, and I gave it to—"

"Stupid talk, Adele. You didn't give him shit except a lesson in blowing bubbles. He died because he was a little killing creep. And you're nothing like him. You killed a monster to protect a little girl. Hell, to protect Paris. To protect others. He didn't deserve the air in his lungs. You just cut the line a bit. Did what our great nation wouldn't. It's tough that some people choose to do evil, but you're nothing like him. Hear me?" He gave her a little shake. "Don't be stupid, Sharp. You did what you had to."

Adele let out a breath, her throat tight. She blinked tears from her eyes, staring at John, trying to see clearly. The bright light above cast his scar in a rigid, harsh light. And yet his eyes were soft, his voice strong, his posture protective.

Was he right? Had she done the right thing?

She didn't think so. He was spinning it, trying to paint her in a better light. But she knew what she'd felt. Knew what she'd done. Knew why she'd done it. According to the DGSI's own enforced laws, she was a criminal. A killer. At the very least, they could fire her. At the very least—

"Stop that," John said, cupping her chin and tilting her head. His fingers were warm against her skin. "Stop that," he said again, more softly. He held her chin, looking her dead in the eyes. "You're not perfect, Adele. I never said that. But you did better than anyone else could've in your own situation. Okay? You did what you had to do. Maybe you made a mistake here or there. Maybe your attitude," he snorted, "wasn't perfect while putting a monster in the grave, but you saved my daughter, you saved others and you stopped a killer. Give yourself a damn break, okay? Stop beating yourself up. You think that's what your mother would've wanted? Robert? Hmm? If anything, the painter wants you to torment yourself. The best way to beat him, and his memory, is to forget him. Bury him beneath neglect and indifference. He doesn't deserve another thought."

Adele didn't look away, preferring to keep her gaze fixated on Renee's. She missed him. Missed the time they so often spent together. She glanced past him towards his house, swallowing. A strange thought—but vaguely, she wondered what it might feel like to live together. To be near him more than a couple times a week, or when they were working a case.

Also, she would never admit it to him, but she felt a bit better.

A faint, lingering residue of guilt still twisted her insides, but John seemed so certain. So confident in what he was saying.

Was he right? Was she needlessly beating herself up?

As if reading her thoughts, John lowered his hand from her chin and glanced off, his own gaze troubled briefly. But then he said, "Look, all of us sometimes do things we don't want to. We do what's right in the wrong way. I get it, I've been there..."

She opened her mouth to speak, but then caught the words, watching him. He seemed on the verge of something, his eyes hooded now, distant. His jaw had tensed, his posture rigid. He was there, but also not there. John only ever got this way when he was thinking back to his military days.

"I—I," he said breathily, stumbling over the words, "I've never told anyone this..." He shot her a look, his eyes laden with something akin to sadness and guilt. "I've had to protect people before, too, Adele. People I cared about. Sometimes it can't be avoided."

Again, Adele didn't speak, stunned. She didn't want to break whatever this spell was that now had John opening up. She wasn't sure what he was going to say, but she'd always been fascinated by the hidden military career of Renee. He'd been French special forces overseas. She knew he'd also been a helicopter pilot and had received his burn wound, the scars along his chest and face, from some horrible accident or attack.

But other than that, he'd always been cagey about his military past.

Now, some of the guilt, the horror, the dreadful anticipation at what she'd come here to say had completely faded to be replaced by stark curiosity. She just waited, watching as Renee swallowed, cleared his throat, then said, "I can't tell you where we were. Just suffice to say there was a lot of damn sand. I hate the sand. I hate the ocean. This place had both shitty things in huge amounts."

Adele winced. She nodded to show she'd heard.

"I—I get what you did, Adele, because I once did the same thing." He gazed off still across the street, away from her, refusing, or perhaps terrified, to meet her gaze. "It was a quiet night. We were on a stealth mission. No talking, no comms—no sounds. Eight of us. Behind enemy lines, on a sabotage mission, got me? I can't really say more."

Adele bobbed her head, watching Renee, wide-eyed. She reached out, stroking his arm. His muscle was tight as steel, his whole body tensed, his eyes shifting wildly now.

"One of the men started having a panic attack. I don't know what triggered it—it was never on his psych eval. We'd been in the same company for nearly five years. He'd never had issues before, but this time, in the final moment, in the dead of night, surrounded by hundreds of enemy insurgents, he started screaming..."

Adele stared. "What—what happened?"

"I tried to calm him. Really, I did... But no use, Adele. He was seeing ghosts. He started shoving, fighting, striking. He thought we were attacking him. He continued to scream, so I was forced to muzzle him. But it didn't stop." He swallowed, his voice hoarse, his eyes haunted. "I had others to worry about. Patrols were starting towards us. I was responsible for everyone's life. We were already exhausted, overburdened. We could hear chatter we'd picked upon the radio. The enemy heard him. They were zeroing in on our location in the dark. Fifteen months of planning, my men—all in jeopardy. He just kept screaming."

"What did you do?"

John closed his eyes, swallowed, then murmured. "He was my

friend, you know? I'd known him for years. We'd even talked about one day opening a small restaurant in Paris together." A ghost of a smile flashed across Renee's cheeks. "But in that moment, he was going to get us all killed. So I struck him. Knocked him unconscious. I put him on my back, determined to carry him out. But too late. They found us."

"The enemy?"

"Fifty men with automatics and RPGs descended on us. In the chaos, I dropped him."

"The man who'd—"

"Yeah. I lost him. Half of my team was killed. No French survived according to the news the next day. The rest of us barely got away with our lives. The mission failed. And he... he never made it back." John sighed, hunched a bit now, eyes staring towards the floorboards of the patio. "I wish I'd thought of something else. I've played that memory over a million times. But I didn't know what else I could do, Adele. If I hadn't knocked him out, the rest of my team might have died, too. If I'd been stronger, if I'd carried him further... But the rocket blasts, the gunfire—I don't even remember when I dropped him. It was night— explosions everywhere. Screaming. By then, other members of my team were dead or shot. I lost track of him. I just left him there. Unconscious, defenseless..." John swallowed. "I—I can only hope they killed him quick when they found him."

"You don't know what happened to him? What was his name?"

John didn't answer this, shaking his head. His hand, she noticed, was trembling, his muscles still tensed.

This time, it was her turn to lean in and give him a hug. "You did the best you could," she murmured.

He sniffed, but looked at her again, now, calming somewhat. He snorted. "Big words. You gonna believe them?"

Adele sighed. She supposed he had her trapped now. "I—maybe you're right," she said softly. "I won't beat myself up if you promise not to."

John snorted. "Too late for that, but I suppose I can stop repeating the process for a bit. Come here, American Princess." He held her again, standing in silence on his porch. City lights from Paris were just visible through the pines lining the sidewalk.

Adele felt safe, standing there. The guilt, the tight knot in her chest was looser. Not gone, but a bit... less.

"I'm glad I came tonight," she murmured.

"I'm glad too, Adele."

She glanced past him, towards the open door of his quaint home.

She peered past him, her mind slowly wandering. Wondering. "John," she said softly.

"Mhmm?"

"I—I was thinking—"

Just then, her phone began to ring.

CHAPTER THREE

A second later, John's phone began to buzz as well. The two ringtones chirped in the night, mingling together on the still air.

John frowned, releasing her. Adele fished her phone from her pocket. "Work?" John said.

She bobbed her head, quickly, lifting the phone. "Yes. You?" Before John could reply, her line connected.

"Agent Sharp?" Executive Foucault's voice chimed out. John's phone, which he'd answered a second late, went quiet. So now, Renee leaned in, trying to listen to Adele's. She turned on the speaker.

"Yes, sir," she said.

"We've got a case. We're contacting John as well."

Adele frowned. "Should we come in?"

"First thing in the morning. Five AM. Don't be late. We're sending you two to Amsterdam."

"How many bodies so far?"

"Two," Foucault said, his voice grim. "One of them a French citizen. DGSI is involving with Interpol on this one. Tomorrow at five sharp. Got it?"

"Yes, sir! I'll tell John as well."

A pause. A cleared throat. "Is he there with you?"

Adele's eyes widened. "Umm, no, sir, I meant I could call him," she said, wincing.

"I see. We'll message him but go ahead and call. We need you on this one. I know it's a bit close to—well, you know. But look, the victims look like you, Adele. It might be useful."

"They what, sir?"

"Look, you'll know more when you get here. Five AM, bright and early. That won't be a problem, will it?"

Adele sighed, clearing her throat but then, her tone as professional as possible, she said, "No sir. We'll be there—er, I mean, I will. I'm sure John will too. If, I mean, when, if I can reach him that is..." Adele panicked, her eyes widening. "I—not that I know where..."

John reached over and hung up.

She stared at her phone, then looked slowly up at John. "Shit," she said.

"Think he knows we're together right now?" John said sarcastically. The big man rolled his eyes. "Shit, indeed. You're a horrible liar, Adele."

"I—I just panicked. I didn't think—"

John leaned in, planted a kiss on her lips, and patted her cheek. "Get some sleep, Sharp. I'll see you bright and early."

Then, he turned, marching back through his front door. He hooked the door behind him with his heel. Adele's eyes lingered on his muscled form as the door slowly shut, then clicked closed.

A second later, the light above the porch turned off, leaving her in darkness.

She frowned towards the door at the sudden, abrupt shift. One moment, John had been conciliatory, then he'd spilled his soul, and now here she was, cold, in the dark, on the other side of the door.

Was he trying to make a point? Or was he serious that he wanted her to get some sleep.

She harrumphed, rolling her eyes, half wanting to march to that door, pound on it until he let her in—damn sleep.

But after a couple of moments of fantasizing, she allowed cooler heads to prevail and, with a long sigh, turned and took the patio steps, moving up the sidewalk, back in the direction of her parked car.

Five AM was early. Especially given how late it was. She supposed a little bit of sleep would go a long way.

She felt lighter as she left Renee's. Part of her was irritated at his abrupt dismissal, another part of her amused. He always seemed to know what to say in the moment, then that done, he'd figure out some new and creative way to piss her off.

She shook her head, muttering beneath her breath, "Damn Frenchman."

Her thoughts sobered a bit as she moved back to the car, frowning now. Her nose was stuffy from crying, her eyes tender. But tears wouldn't matter in the morning.

Two victims, he'd said. One of them French. She hadn't been to Amsterdam before... The city's reputation preceded it.

So why was there a killer in Amsterdam? And what had Foucault meant by that last part...

The victims look like you, Adele...

She felt another faint shiver as the wind picked up, and her pace quickened as she hurried towards her parked car under the watchful gaze of night.

***

Adele's phone rang as she yawned, gripping the steering wheel of her rental, and navigating the circling ramp of the parking structure outside DGSI headquarters. Behind, in the rearview mirror, she spotted the pink painted café nestled against the base of the taller building. The air smelled faintly of paint, as it had for the last few years ever since the renovations.

She glanced down at the screen beneath her. Her phone connected to the vehicle. Her father was calling.

Adele winced, yawning again and placing a hand over her mouth; she pulled up the ramp to the third floor of the parking structure.

Ahead, through sliding glass doors, she spotted the security checkpoint into the building.

The clock above the radio told her she had five minutes to spare before she was due to meet with John in the executive's office.

Normally, she would have waited to field a call within such close parameters. But things were going well with the Sergeant. Her father had softened ever since the death of his ex-wife's killer. She didn't want to risk offending him, so as she pulled between the two white painted lines, she reached over and clicked the phone symbol on the screen.

Instantly, she heard the crackle of the device connecting. Then, the Sergeant's voice. "Adele? Can you hear me? To hell with this all. Why can't I hear you? No, wait. There we go." He accidentally hung up.

Adele sighed faintly, waiting for the inevitable redial. Again, the car echoed with the generic ringtone. She answered again, and this time spoke first. "I can hear you, Dad. Can you hear me?"

"There you are," her father said, grunting. "I hate this stuff, Adele. Technology is going to be the death of me."

She smirked, grateful that he couldn't see her on video.

"How's it going Dad?"

"Fine, fine."

"You're up early," she said.

He grunted. "Win the morning, win the day."

"Fair enough. Thanks for calling."

"I saw you called a couple of days ago. Is everything all right?"

Adele hesitated and bit the corner of her lip. Her father had returned to Germany not long after she'd killed the painter. He had stayed with her for a bit following the incident, looking after her, keeping her company. Now, back in Germany, he sounded more chipper than normal.

She felt a flash of guilt. Was she doing her father wrong by not telling him what had actually happened in the park? He still believed it was self-defense. It hadn't gone nearly as horribly as expected when telling John. Maybe her father would be in a forgiving mood too...

She hesitated, wincing, but then lost her nerve and covered by saying, "Sorry about that. I was just calling to see how you were doing after the flight. Did you get in okay?"

He gave a noncommittal grunt. "Fine, fine." She pictured him pulling at his walrus mustache, his thick forearms crossed over his small belly.

"I actually had to come in to work early," she said. "Think we could call later this week? Maybe we could watch one of those shows you like so much over the phone."

She winced as she said it. Never in the past would she have recommended watching a TV show while on the phone together. To her surprise, though, her father didn't scoff at the suggestion. Instead, he said, "Might be fun. Let me check to see if anything good is on. I won't keep you from work. Priorities. I'll talk to you later. Have a good day, dear."

And then he hung up. But Adele just sat, stunned. Had her father called her *dear*?

What was happening? She felt a lance of guilt. She needed to tell him, didn't she? Tell him what had really happened...

She suppressed this thought, shaking her head and pushing out of the car. Things would have to wait on that front. It was early, she was in a sour mood, and the last thing she wanted was for Agent Renee to beat her to the executive's office. As much as she liked John, there was always a miniature competition between them at work. They had both been athletic as kids. They liked the competition. And Adele refused to reach the executive's office last. She picked up the pace, hurrying across the concrete parking lot towards the security checkpoint beyond the glass doors.

Part of her wanted to beat John, but another part of her was intrigued. What did the executive mean about the victims resembling her?

***

John had beaten her to the office. She tried not to look too sullen as she crossed her arms, sitting across the large oak table where the executive reclined, glaring at them from beneath a hawk-like brow over a bold, Roman nose. The room no longer smelled of cigarette smoke. It had taken months for the candles and scent strips to completely absorb the residue of the bad habit.

Now, a small pile of nicotine gum wrappers collected on his desk. Foucault chewed thoughtfully as he glanced with his dark gaze between the two agents.

"I'm glad both of you could make it so quickly," he said. He didn't sound sarcastic, and yet there was something about his tone. Or maybe it was just the way he kept looking between the two of them. Office romance was discouraged. They had never officially declared a relationship, and she saw no reason to start now.

The executive crossed his arms. He leaned back in his leather chair. "Files are texted to your emails," he said. "Two victims so far. Both of them prostitutes. Both strangled to death."

John perked up at the word *prostitute*. Adele scowled at the word *strangled*.

"One of the women was Belgian, the other French. Interpol is coordinating, and we're assigned to the task. I'm sending you to Amsterdam, to the red-light district, and I'm advising you up front: I need you both to play nice. You might be in another country, but we're going to abide by agency protocol. Clear?"

At this last part he was staring straight at John. He waited, impatiently.

John blinked, looking surprised. "Of course," he said his voice a bit too high pitched.

Adele shot her boyfriend an angry glare. He had created a reputation for himself as somewhat of a womanizer but had reigned it in ever since dating Adele. Still, she would keep a close eye on him in Amsterdam. She believed in the principle of *trust but verify.*

"You mentioned something about the victims resembling me," Adele said, frowning.

The executive nodded. "Check the files. It's all in there. Look, we have no reason to think that the killer is slowing down. So far he's struck over the last two days. Two bodies in forty-eight hours, which is an issue. As I'm sure you know. On top of that, he's a ghost. Which is why they're calling in our help."

Adele leaned forward, frowning. "What do you mean ghost?"

"He's not leaving any DNA evidence behind. No traces, no fibers, no fluids. His face isn't being picked up on the cameras. There's no sign of this killer. As you might imagine, we're trying to avoid turning this into a spectacle. Amsterdam has a reputation of its own, but we don't need to tarnish that too thoroughly. Understand?"

John shot a look at Adele. "Politics?" He guessed.

The executive scowled. "Let me worry about politics. You do your job. Find this killer. Find out how he's avoiding detection. And catch him before he kills again. Got it?"

Both agents nodded.

"Your flight leaves in an hour. You should get going."

***

Adele sat cramped in the window seat next to John Renee. He had conquered the armrests and she was too tired to put up much of a fight. Besides, most of her attention was captured by the case file open on her laptop. The airplane shuddered briefly as they hit a patch of turbulence, and behind her, Adele heard one of the other passengers gasp. She'd flown so often, Adele barely even noticed.

John was leaning over, also looking at the case file as Adele scrolled through.

"A prostitute from Amsterdam," John said with a low whistle. "It's like the holy grail."

"Don't be a weirdo."

"I'm not. I'm just saying. You hear stories. Not that I would ever participate," he added quickly, shooting her a sidelong glance.

Adele rolled her eyes. "John, if I ever find you cheating on me with a prostitute, I'm going to call up Agent Leoni so quickly it will make your head spin."

John scowled at the reference to the handsome, Italian agent. He snapped, "All right, no need to get nasty. Point taken."

"Besides, have a little decorum. These women are dead."

John shook his head. "You're prettier anyway," he muttered.

Adele smiled, but hid it, glancing at the photos of the two women. Both of them blonde. Both of them pretty, and tall. Adele herself was as tall as most men, at five-foot-nine.

She frowned towards the pictures, pressing a hand through her own dark, blonde hair.

"The killer has a type."

"Tall, blonde prostitutes," John said. "Not exactly a needle in a haystack. There will be a lot of people that fit that description in Amsterdam. Gonna be nearly impossible to find employment records at places like these anyway. Discretion matters."

"True. Have you ever been to De Wallen's red-light district before?"

"Never been to Amsterdam. The trip never came up, I guess. I hear it's a tourist trap. But a very enjoyable tourist trap."

Adele scrolled down the pictures, studying the report. Both of them strangled with a silk scarf. This was the only thing they'd found fibers from. The scarf was taken after the murder. There were no prints. No semen. No saliva. No sign of sexual assault. No physical evidence whatsoever. Just a body left on a bed. Something else was interesting that Adele had noticed. The killer seemed to be posing the women. Not in any sort of grotesque fashion. Rather, he placed their hands at their sides, smoothed their outfits, and then covered them with blankets, as if attempting to preserve their modesty. He killed them, then covered them. He would leave their faces exposed, as if worried they might suffocate. Strange. Very strange.

John was talking about prostitutes again, and Adele decided now was a good time to battle for the armrest. She zeroed in with an elbow, aiming for his ribs, and when he reacted she conquered the divider.

She ignored his protest, feeling a sense of justice.

In Adele's reckoning there was nothing awe-inspiring about prostitution. She knew too many victims involved in the business. Killers often targeted prostitutes because they determined no one would miss them. This killer was wrong. Adele was determined to stop him.

CHAPTER FOUR

The taxi from the airport took them to the latest crime scene. Adele reclined in the back seat, her eyes wide as she stared through the window at the Red Light District of De Wallen. A huge tourist hub of a city strip, boasting clubs, bars, restaurants, shops—not to mention the hundreds of brothels and women dancing slowly in gaudily lit windows alongside bollard-lined waterways. Some tourists did their best to only look askance towards the women as they moved past, but other windows had gaggles of onlookers ogling the dancers.

For his part, Agent Renee, sitting in the front seat, was staring determinedly at his phone, pretending he wasn't interested in the least by the scantily clad visual presentations.

"First time in Amsterdam?" the taxi driver asked in perfect English, quirking a bushy eyebrow in the rearview mirror.

Adele glanced towards him, giving a quick nod. She cleared her throat, "Say, do you know anything about the Red Letter brothel?"

The driver nodded once. "Only a few more blocks," he said congenially.

"No, sorry, that's not what I meant. Do you know anything about the place itself—the clients, the workers?"

He shrugged once. "I'm not sure what you want to know. It is a mid-level establishment. Never been there myself."

"Sorry," Adele repeated, "I wasn't implying any—well, just, is it known for any incidents? Criminal activity?"

Now the taxi driver looked somewhat bemused. "Criminal activity? I heard there was some unfortunate incident with one of the ladies yesterday."

"Right," Adele said. "Anything else?"

He shrugged. "I am happily married." He raised his hand, wiggling his fingers and displaying the ring. "I don't visit these places. Besides," he added, waving the same ringed hand towards the many women in windows along the streets. "It would be impossible to keep track of *all* the news from all these places."

Adele gave a faint sigh. "I'm getting worried about that," she muttered. "Thank you," she added in a livelier tone.

Inwardly, though, as she stared along the streets and their taxi carried them deeper into the heart of De Wallen, Adele felt a lingering sense of unease.

With so many brothels, so many sex-workers, so many tourists, it was going to be a nightmare to try and zero in on the killer's next victim or the killer himself.

Tracking brothel clients was difficult to begin with, but in a tourist destination, so many people were coming and going it would be nearly impossible to trace every witness, to track every suspect, to even locate the relevant parties.

This case, Adele felt certain, was going to be a headache.

"Ah, here we are!" the driver exclaimed. "Have fun, you two!"

He pulled to a practiced halt with a flourish of the steering wheel next to a clean window with tastefully arranged fairy lights. No dancer here, just painted letters which said *Red Letter.* Below, in neat type, the establishment's hours were displayed next to a small, laminated sticky note with a bright, pink smiley face and a picture of a video camera.

Adele glanced up through the window and spotted the blinking red light above the entrance.

John was already pushing out of the cramped cab to stretch his long legs. With a weary sigh and an already forming headache, Adele paid the driver then joined him on the sidewalk, facing the brothel.

A young police officer was standing outside the door, fidgeting nervously, and glancing as John and Adele moved up the sidewalk, towards the entrance. Adele's eyes flicked up, noting the blinking red light above.

The young cop stepped aside, using his arm to open the glass doorway. He cleared his throat, and, in lightly accented English, he said, "The woman was found on the second floor."

Agent Renee scowled, reaching into his pocket and raising his DGSI ID. "Usually protocol to check these things," he said.

The young cop stammered, gaping like a fish, but then John just smirked, patted him on the shoulder and sidled past, muttering, "Then again, there doesn't seem to be much of *any* protocol in this place."

Adele winced apologetically as she also stepped into the brothel. Red candle lights were situated in small alcoves up a row of stairs. The scent of cinnamon and other melting wax odors wafted through the hall. Sunlight gleamed through windows with colored glass, spotlighting the agents as they took the stairs.

"I'm guessing the proprietors have closed the place?" Adele said faintly.

"Umm, no—no, not at all. Workers will be coming through in a few hours for the evening."

Adele shot the young officer a look, and he gave a faint wince. "Time is money," he added by way of explanation. "Here, the body was found in this room."

They had reached the second floor, and he knocked a hand against a wooden door. The frame creaked slowly open, revealing a similarly scented, similarly lit, cozy bedroom. The body had long since been removed, but caution tape closed off the bed and the shower.

The cop pointed towards the edge of the bed. "Victim was found there."

"This is a private room?" Adele asked, stepping onto the squishy carpet and peering around the small space. She frowned towards another candle in an alcove, her eyes moving towards an open door beyond the bed revealing a bathroom.

"Yes, private," the cop said. "According to the proprietors and the madam on duty that night, the killer came in as an ordinary client."

"And strangled her with a scarf," Adele said. "I read the report." She faced the bed, picturing the crime scene photos she'd gone through. Flashes of images of an attractive, blonde woman, glassy-eyed, staring sightless at the ceiling, her neck twisted, her body collapsed on itself.

"We did not find the murder weapon," the officer said. "Are we sure it was a scarf?"

Adele drummed her fingers on her thigh, catching the back of her phone through the thin fabric. "Yes," she murmured. "Fibers found. Most likely some type of scarf according to the coroner... Why would the killer take it with him?"

She dropped to the ground, suddenly, peering beneath the bed, holding her breath so as to not inhale the odor from the floor.

She scanned the underside of the bed but frowned further. Nothing. Just... clean. Strangely clean for a place like this. She pushed back to her feet. "Nothing broken," she murmured. "No mess. No struggle. The blankets aren't even off the bed."

John grunted. "She must have let him put the scarf around her neck willingly. A sex game gone too far, perhaps?"

Adele let out a faint sigh. "If not for that other victim...," she trailed off.

The cop by the door stiffened as they spoke. He said, "There are strict guidelines in many of these places. All the girls are vetted and tested..."

"Are there similar guidelines for the clients?" Adele asked.

"Umm... Some. But they don't have to provide ID. They prefer discretion. In most locations they don't take names or keep records."

"I spotted a camera at the front door."

"Ah, well, yes," the cop said, nodding. "We had the footage sent last night."

"You have that footage?"

"I believe so—it's not my department. But there are a lot of clients and hours and hours of that stuff to go through. So, I'm sure if anything comes up—"

Adele turned, speaking curtly. "I'd like to see that footage for myself."

"I can take you to the precinct," he said, carefully. "But you may have to wait a couple hours for the proper—"

"No need," John grunted, shoving past the cop and pushing back into the hall. "Hello?" John bellowed at the top of his lungs. "Who is here? Hello!"

The cop just stared uneasily at John. Adele sighed, approaching the big man in the hall. She'd grown accustomed to John's sudden epiphanies followed by bursts of action. She'd long since learned to simply let them run their course. Agent Renee's career was Teflon.

"Hello!" John called louder.

A pause. Then, a faint, worried voice. "I—yes?"

"Bingo," John muttered, clicking his fingers and pointing up the hall towards a metal door just visible past a bend. "Camera over that door, too. See?"

Adele did, spotting another blinking red light facing the hall.

"The owners live there," the cop said hurriedly. "We already questioned them. Best not to disturb—"

"I'm already disturbed," Adele said. She followed John's lead as he stalked up the hall and approached the sealed metal door. A big fist raised, preparing to pound on the door, but before it could, a crack appeared in the metal. A groan, a sound of a chain, and the door opened, revealing two, short, plump and smiling denizens. A middle-aged man with a comb-over and a gray-haired woman with shaded glasses.

John lowered his hand where he'd been about to knock and flashed an easygoing smile with a quick tap of his fingers to his forehead in a mock bow. "I was wondering who'd stayed behind to babysit. So you two own this place, is that right?"

The cop behind them protested weakly, apologizing emphatically. "I'm very sorry, Mr. and Mrs. Carmen—I tried to tell them you didn't want to be disturbed."

But Mrs. Carmen didn't seem to hear him. She was too busy admiring John's imposing physique. "My, my," she said in flawless English. "You are a big one." Her hand lifted suddenly, tapping the underside of John's chin, tracing his scar down towards his chest. "Pity that," she said. "If not for the burn, you would've been quite the prize."

John gave a little snort of offense, pushing the woman's hand away. Before her partner could say anything equally damaging, Adele stepped in, interjecting, "Apologies, but we were wondering if we could check the footage." She pointed towards the camera above the door.

Mrs. Carmen frowned, retracting her hand. "We already provided a copy of the film to the police."

"We'd like to see it firsthand," Adele said. "We're with DGSI, but working with Interpol."

"French!" the woman exclaimed. "I love the French—ah, my. Poor Silver *was* French."

"The victim?"

"Yes, yes... I have her ID somewhere... one moment, one moment." Mrs. Carmen turned and moved towards a large, black safe against the far wall under a third security camera. She spun the lock, blocking it with her body and shawl, and after a moment, opened the safety compartment. She rummaged through the safe for a few moments, and then emerged, with a faint squeal of anguish, waving a rectangle of plastic over her head. "Here it is," she said, her voice melancholy all of a sudden. "I'm telling you, Silver was just the best. I'm going to miss her so very much."

Adele frowned as the woman returned to the door. "You didn't give this to the police?"

"This? It's a copy. I don't have her actual ID. And I *did* provide a second copy to my nephew, Henry, here."

The young cop in the hall winced at this comment.

"Nephew?" John snorted.

Henry just blushed, clearing his throat and looking off to the side. Adele was once again reminded that things would be done differently in De Wallen. She cleared her throat, extending a hand courteously to accept the copied ID.

Mrs. Carmen obliged and then said to her husband, "Dennis, mind fetching that footage for us again, dear?"

The older man smiled, displaying a gap-toothed grin, and nodded once. Without saying a word, he turned and moved down a hall, disappearing from view.

"He'll just be a moment," Mrs. Carmen whispered. "He's gotten slow in his old age... Though, not in bed. If you know what I mean." She wiggled her painted on eyebrows and elbowed John playfully in the midriff.

Adele was too busy to check if John was blushing. She held the copy of the ID up to the light, frowning. "This is fake," she said simply.

"Excuse me?"

"The ID, ma'am—it's a forgery. Is this the only one she gave you?"

"I—well, I never... why would she give me a fake ID?"

Adele shrugged and wiggled the piece of plastic. "Mind if I keep this?"

"Of course, of course. I have another." Mrs. Carmen's fake eyebrows drooped now, and she scowled. "So odd," she said. "Why would Silver lie?"

Adele was wondering this very thing. But before she could posit a theory, Mr. Carmen returned, shuffling and holding a large tablet between his gnarled fingers. It took an age and a half for him to navigate his way around a sleek dining room table, and an expensive television set. Finally, when he arrived at the door, he was panting faintly and extended the device towards the agents.

John took it, spinning it and scanning the screen.

"Three angles from yesterday," Mrs. Carmen advised. She pointed towards three rectangular buttons in the top left. She leaned in, a bit too closely to John, brushing up against him, and smiling coyly. "Here, one moment," she murmured huskily.

John leaned away, but Mrs. Carmen fast-forwarded the cameras and then clicked her tongue. "There we go," she said happily. "The client who hurt Silver is right there—the one in the hat. See him?"

Adele and John leaned in now, studying the screen.

John clicked the rectangular button at the top left as he'd been instructed, and the view shifted to the hallway they were currently standing in. A few seconds passed, and the same man appeared at the end of the hall.

"He's ducking his head," John growled.

Adele had noticed the same thing. The killer's hat obscured his features. He wore an overcoat which hid his form. He slouched a bit to hide his height.

"He knows where the cameras are," Adele said faintly. "This wasn't just a sex game gone wrong. It wasn't heat of the moment. He planned this."

John frowned. "That means he came here for *this* girl. He wasn't targeting a hooker. He was targeting *this* woman." He tapped the ID still cupped in Adele's hands.

They replayed the footage a couple more times, but the killer knew his stuff. He moved cautiously, his features perfectly hidden.

"He's done this before," Adele murmured. "Maybe more than once." She thought of the first victim—the Belgian. What if she *wasn't* the first?

A faint shiver went down Adele's spine, and she surreptitiously glanced at the photo ID. A pretty woman, with off-blonde hair. Tall, somewhat exotic features.

Foucault seemed to think Adele resembled the victims. She wasn't sure she saw it personally, but this just added another concern to her already growing list.

"I think we should visit the brothel where the Belgian was killed," John said, turning to look back down the hall.

Adele sighed, nodding, and she handed the tablet back to Mr. Carmen. Bidding their farewells, they moved back down the hall. Adele kept glancing over her shoulder towards the blinking light.

Were they missing something? The killer had come here, targeting this prostitute specifically. Why?

And why had she lied about being French?

The first victim might help connect the dots. Adele wasn't ecstatic about visiting another murder scene in another brothel, but she'd known this case wouldn't be a particularly pleasant one. Then again, when were they ever?

CHAPTER FIVE

He adjusted his tie nervously, feeling the sweat prickling along his forehead. He smoothed his hair quickly with one hand and checked his breath against the back of his wrist. With trembling fingers, he pulled a tube of mints from his pocket, popped one, and resettled in his seat by the bar.

He barely even noticed the pulsing, strobing lights from the dance floor. Normally, he wasn't one given to patronizing nightclubs. But for her? He'd move mountains.

Still—where the hell was she?

He adjusted his glasses, smoothing his hair once more. His eyes kept darting across the room and inevitably flitting towards the door. A small twang of a guitar string, the sound the door made whenever it opened. A flash of blonde hair. A pale, smiling face.

His heart pounded; he nearly crushed his glasses. But then as he peered towards the approaching woman, his stomach fell. No—not her. The approaching lady leaned between two friends, laughing loudly, already half-drunk it seemed.

He hid his sneer of contempt. *She* never would have gotten drunk. Never did. He didn't remember the last time he'd seen her drink.

He didn't partake either. He glanced towards the small water sitting on his circular table, and bowed his head, sighing a faint breath. The strobing lights, the loud music—he hated the nightclub. But he'd go anywhere to find her. He'd already proven that, hadn't he?

Off to the side, he knew one of the cameras was recording. He made sure to direct his face in such a way to avoid being spied on by the eye in the sky.

Soon, though, none of it would matter.

He'd find her. That's all he'd ever wanted. The one that got away.

But not forever—he would have his happy ending. She would be a part of it. His eyes misted a bit at the thought of a sailing off into the sunset. He pulled a length of silk cloth from his chest pocket, wrapping it around and around his fingers.

As soft as the day he remembered it.

He let the scarf uncurl and flutter briefly from the over-zealous vent above his head. The chill blast of air conditioning tried to accommodate for all the sweaty, horny, tipsy bodies moving about the club.

He folded the scarf, placing it back in his pocket. His eyes moved across the dancers, searching, always searching. But still no sign of her. He hadn't missed her yet. She had yet to arrive.

This was fine. He was patient—he'd always been patient. It was one of his greatest skills. He'd waited a long time to find her again, hadn't he?

He could wait a few more minutes... hours... whatever it took.

Whatever the cost.

CHAPTER SIX

John and Adele stood in a far sleazier bedroom this time. The scent was of talcum powder and regret. No candles here. No mood-lighting. Even the door was moldered, with a quick covering of paint attempting to hide the water damage. The carpets alone made Adele's stomach turn.

She stared at the phone in John's hand as he cycled through the crime scene photos before the body had been removed.

"Only a short time before our fake Frenchwoman," John said quietly. "He definitely has a type."

Adele frowned at the photo on the screen in John's hand. Another blonde woman, more homely features, but not unattractive. Marie Dubois. She was also tall. Belgian, though. This ID checked out.

She heard the incessant tap of knuckles against the closed door behind them.

"We need the room!" shouted the bouncer who'd reluctantly allowed them into the brothel.

"We're not done yet!" Adele called back.

More insistent, angry knocking.

"Do that again, and we'll shut the whole place down!" John bellowed.

This was more effective. The knocking stopped, though Adele did hear a faint series of dark mutterings and the sound of retreating footsteps.

She glanced back, making sure the door was still closed, then returned her attention, in the moldy, dingy bedroom, to the phone in John's hand as he pulled up the coroner's report. "Same story," Adele said, her eyes skipping down the block of text she'd already memorized on the way over. "Strangulation. Not by rope, too soft. Best guess is a scarf or some type of bed sheet."

John shook his head. "Bedsheets in the photos were all beneath the body."

"And no scarfs," Adele replied. She glanced around the room, moving over to a small radiator, and peering behind it. More water damage, but no hidden murder weapons. "He took it with him again," she concluded.

"Why? What does the scarf mean to him?"

"What do these women mean," she returned. "Blonde—pretty..."

"Hookers?"

"That could describe hundreds in this city," Adele said with a faint moan. She rounded on John once more, giving a helpless little shrug. "Think this place has cameras?"

"Didn't see any on the way in."

"What about across the street?"

John shook his head. "You notice any?"

Adele sighed. "No—I'm guessing in a place like this," she sniffed in disgust, "Privacy is sort of the point."

"Well... might not have cameras," John said slowly, "But we do have witnesses..."

Adele paused, then gave a faint shrug. "Usually this crowd is somewhat tight-lipped. But it's not like the bouncer can get any more pissed. We can speak to anyone who was working that evening—when was it again?"

"Tuesday."

"Right... Anyone working Tuesday evening. They might know something."

"Hookers have long memories," John said, a flash of fear in his eyes. He shook his head quickly. "Not—er, not that I'd know."

"Sure, John. Whatever." Adele marched past him "accidentally" elbowing him in the gut. The sound of air whooshing from the big man was somewhat satisfying as she pushed open the door handle and immediately felt an urge to wash her hands.

She called down the hall, "Excuse me—yes, you, sir."

"Done with the room?" the bouncer demanded.

"Umm, no, in fact. We're not quite done yet. We need to speak to some of the girls."

The balding man with the beer gut glared at them. "Impossible."

John cleared his throat, massaging his stomach. "We can always just shut the place down—"

"Fine!" the bouncer snapped. "Who? Names?"

"We don't have names. Just girls who were working Tuesday in the evening. Can you do that?"

The bouncer ran a meaty hand over his sweaty head, but sighed, snorted, and turned without comment, marching back down the hall. Adele glanced towards John, who shrugged. They started to move after the pitbull-looking man, but he came to a halt by a door with a peeling sign that read "Dressing Room."

He pounded his fist against the door, shouting. "Guests!" Then he kicked the door open and gestured angrily at it. "Go on," he snapped. "You're wasting our time."

Adele winced apologetically, but John just snorted, marching towards the open door. "Thank you," he said primly as he sidled past the man's beer gut.

Adele followed after the Frenchman, her thoughts clouding once more with considerations of the motive behind the killings. Two women dead in quick succession. Prostitutes. The killer had hidden his identity. Known about the cameras.

This was planned. He was targeting specific people. How many more names were on his list? How many more would be crossed off before they caught up with him?

In a place like De Wallen, it would be easy to lose track of a needle in a haystack.

CHAPTER SEVEN

Adele couldn't help but notice some of the women hadn't done much to preserve their modesty as the two agents entered the dressing room through the open door. Agent Renee's cheeks had taken on an odd tinge as they moved through a long, rectangular room filled with large mirrors. Adele counted five women, lounging on seats, adjusting their outfits or attending to their makeup.

A couple of the women shot John looks and leaned in to giggle something in one another's ears. Another woman, the oldest of the bunch, pulled a shawl across her shoulders, and studied the two agents with the severest of expressions.

"How may we help you?" this woman said, standing to her feet all of a sudden. Besides the shawl, she wore a sleek, red dress, parted at the right hip. She wore minimal makeup, and her hair had two curlers in it over her bangs.

The mirror behind her displayed the open, plunging V of the back of the dress.

Adele shifted uncomfortably where she stood in John's shadow, her eyes darting around. The door to the dressing room closed slowly, and she heard the faint sound of voices as the bouncer greeted another customer with the words, "She'll be right with you. Your room is this way—come."

The voices trailed off and Adele met the gaze of the woman in the red dress. "We don't mean to take up your time," she said quickly, "but we're here about Marie Dubois. She went by Margaret."

The giggling from the two younger women suddenly died. The woman in the dress frowned, but quickly adjusted her expression and dabbed a finger beneath her eye as if checking her foundation. "A very sad thing," this woman said. "Who are you?"

"My name is Agent Sharp. This is Agent Renee. We're working the case."

"You're not from De Wallen." It wasn't a question.

"No, we're with Interpol. DGSI."

"Ah, French. Marie was Belgian. I'm surprised they'd send the French." She crossed her arms, accentuating her chest. John cleared his throat but pressed on courageously.

"Were any of you working Tuesday night, when she was killed?" John said, glancing around the room.

No one raised their hand. No one said anything.

"You're not in trouble," Adele hastily added. "We're looking for a description. Anyone who might have seen the man."

Again, a row of blank looks. But then, one of the younger women sitting by the large mirrors volunteered. "He was unremarkable," she said. "I remember him."

"You do? What can you tell us?" Adele asked quickly.

This woman had red hair—dyed most likely—and was wearing a nightgown. She crossed her legs delicately, the motion clearly the result of lots of practice. She sat primly and folded her hands over her crooked knee. "He was with Marie—I remember that much. He was adamant it had to be her."

"He requested her personally?"

"Yes."

"And you saw him?"

The woman gave a graceful little shrug. "Like I said—I barely noticed him. I just remember him insisting he spend the night with her. I was also on call." She sniffed, running a hand through her hair. "It was quite offensive, in fact."

"So you don't remember anything about the man, besides he was unremarkable? What height? Hair color? Age?"

She just shrugged, shaking her head and pursing her lips. "I don't remember."

Adele felt a surge of frustration but didn't let it show. Instead, she tried a different track. "Did you notice anything else about that night?" She glanced around at the other women. A few shaken heads, more blank expressions. Adele could feel her frustration now mounting.

John half raised a hand, as if he were in school, then, embarrassed, jammed the hand into his pocket. As if to accommodate the faux pas, he said, in a gruff voice, "You gotta help us somehow, ladies. Anything you can think of might make the difference. Could've been one of you."

"Not likely," said the woman in the red dress. "I don't do BDSM, sugar. But I might make an exception for you."

More giggling from the two by the mirror.

Adele said, "Did you have a sense of regulars who were into that sort of thing? Bondage, choking—anything like that?"

The woman shook her head. "Not my area. Matilda?"

A woman who'd remained quiet up to this point, with springy, dark hair shifted uncomfortably behind a row of clothing where she'd been trying to make herself scarce. She shifted some of the hangers, as if perusing, then sighed. "Some regulars—no one like that. No one dangerous. And as for Marie—no." She shrugged and went quiet. Then added quickly, "Privacy is important in this business. Discretion is the best way to *get* repeat clients. Marie didn't give away specific details. She wanted the business."

"What about that skinny man, though," said a woman by the mirror, shaking her head. "You talked about him long enough!"

"That was different!" Matilda protested. "He was a freak!"

A few of the other women glared and nodded with this assessment.

"Excuse me?" Adele interjected. "So there is someone?"

The woman behind the coat rack said, bouncing her dark curls off to the side as if clearing her gaze. "There was this one guy; he's banned now. But he came in a few times a few months ago. Didn't want sex, just wanted to hold and cuddle the girls for a while. He was with Marie—umm, Margaret I mean, one night—I remember that."

"Oh? So you do remember some of her clients?"

"This one, yes. He tried the same shit with me the previous week." Her fingers trailed to the gentle slope of her neck, massaging faintly.

"Tried what?" John said.

Matilda sniffed. "He just wanted to cuddle, but he got rough. I sent him scramming. The next week he books with Marie. She's a bit more forgiving than me... Well, she was." Matilda's eyes narrowed. "And look where it got her."

"This man attacked Marie?" John pressed.

Matilda sighed. "He was just on the bed with her. His time was up but he refused to let her go. I could hear the shouting from the next room. Finn broke in quick enough, but I also went to see what was happening. Even with security there, the skinny man just kept squeezing. He refused to let go. He squeezed so tight he cut her air off. It took Finn and Erol nearly a minute to pull him off." She tapped her fingers on the metal bar of the clothing rack. "It caused a really big scene. The sort of scene we don't like around here."

"Police?" Adele guessed.

Matilda sniffed but gave a quick nod which received a glare from the woman in the red dress.

A fist suddenly banged on the door. "Alright!" the bouncer called. "Back to work. Clients are waiting. Come on ladies!"

Adele stepped aside as a couple of the women hurried out of the room. She shared a look with John, both of them likely thinking the same thing.

If the police had been called to arrest a violent "john," then they'd have information on file. The workers at the brothel might not keep names or addresses, but the police would.

And if this man had tried to strangle Marie a few months ago, who was to say he didn't finish the job. Next stop would be the police station. Adele didn't want to admit it too loudly, but she was glad to be leaving the brothels for the time being.

CHAPTER EIGHT

The police station was on the second floor of an office building. A strange location, Adele thought, as she and John rounded the banister with tapping footsteps on the marble stairs. Two glass, double doors swung at the end of the hall as John shouldered his way in.

Adele scanned the entrance room, her eyes flitting around the space. If she'd thought she could escape the prostitutes by coming here, she'd been mistaken. The business of the town also crept into its police station. One woman was sitting in a short skirt on a greasy bench with an ice pack over a bruised eye while a man, being led away in handcuffs, was shouting curses at her.

Another woman was standing by the front desk, filling out forms, a fur scarf draped over her bare shoulders.

Adele sighed, clearing her throat. Her eyes landed on a familiar face of a figure behind the counter.

"Henry!" she called towards the young officer who'd shown them the second victim's location. "Hey, officer!"

The cop glanced over, and then winced. He stowed something in a sliding cabinet and then hurried over towards the edge of the counter where John and Adele were trying not to crowd the woman in the fur shawl.

"Umm, hello," Officer Henry Jansen said, furtively glancing from Adele to John. "Did you visit the second location?"

"We did," Adele said, "and found something interesting." She lowered her voice, turning her back on the woman filling out the report behind her. The man in cuffs was still shouting as a couple of officers tried to shove him like a fish into a can of sardines through a metal door in the back of the precinct.

Officer Jansen glanced over, winced, and looked back. "What did you find?"

"Another john," Adele said, "apparently from a few months ago tried to strangle Marie Dubois. He had a run in with another prostitute as well."

"Ah—I see. Was a police report filed..." he trailed off and sighed. "That's why you're here?"

"Bingo," John said, slapping a hand against the marble counter.

"We need to see what you have on the charges."

"Alright, alright. One moment. Look, we have a spare interrogation room back this way. Might be a bit less noisy." With quick, furtive motions, he gestured at the two of them to follow after him around the side of the counter. He unlocked a metal door with a bulletproof glass frame, and then gestured for them to follow along the hall and into a small interrogation room with a couple of cold, metal chairs and a plastic table padlocked to the floor.

As John and Adele entered the room, Officer Jansen rounded on them, clicking the door shut with his heel. "So what would you like to know?" he asked with a tilt of his head.

Adele hesitated. "Umm, we'd like to see the arrest report on—"

"No arrest report."

"Wait—what? But you just said—"

Henry passed a hand over his face, massaging his chin. "I was the one who took the call," he said.

"You keep popping up at these locations," Agent Renee interjected. "Anything to do with that aunt of yours?"

Jansen scowled. "Yes, in fact. My aunt runs a brothel. It wouldn't have been my first choice for her employment. But it does give me something of a window into that world. They trust me. Oftentimes they'll ask for me personally."

"Is that what happened on this call?"

Jansen nodded, still standing in the doorway which had closed behind him. "Yes," he said. "I went, took the man's information, but no one wanted to pursue any charges. It's not unheard of—how do you think other clients would feel if they heard a man was arrested at a brothel?"

"For choking someone," Adele pointed out.

"It wouldn't look like that. These are businesses, whatever else you might think of them. They have to keep their clients in mind."

"You sound like you approve," John said.

"I'm sympathetic, that's all. Like I said, they didn't press charges—there is no arrest report. Besides, I knew the man. He'd also had a bit of an incident at my aunt's place, too."

Adele's eyebrows shot up. She took a step closer to the officer. "Seriously? This mysterious strangler was also at the Red Letter?"

"Yes—mostly harmless. A bit unstable. I told him to stay away from both locations. Haven't heard from him since."

"I don't think you're listening, sir. This man assaulted a prostitute by choking her, and also had an incident at your aunt's place. That means he's connected to both crime scenes. Don't you think that might be relevant?"

"Ah, Mr. Osloo didn't kill those women."

"Mr. Osloo?" Adele said, jumping on the name.

"I—umm, yes. That's—like I said I took his information. He wasn't an unfamiliar face to me. I've had to drag him away from more than one bar in the past. He's a troublemaker, but harmless."

"Does this harmless man have an address?"

Officer Jansen hesitated, but then loosed a long sigh. "Yes, of course. Just—just don't tell him I sent you."

Renee shot a look of incredulity only Adele caught. She tried to keep her own thoughts to herself. But it was quite odd, the way the policeman was acting. As if he cared more about preserving the reputation of his aunt's business than actually helping them find a killer.

"You do at least have some kind of report, don't you?" Adele said at last, frowning at Jansen.

"Yes, yes of course. It might take some finding. I don't know if I remembered to file it electronically yet. Just-just hang tight." The man shifted nervously, glancing between the two agents but then with a sigh pushed back through the door and out into the noisy police station.

The door slowly swung shut behind him.

Adele turned, raising an eyebrow in Renee's direction.

"Didn't realize prostitutes had a PR team," John murmured, partly in humor and partly in irritation. He snorted and ran his hand through his dark, slick hair. "Unbelievable."

"I suppose things are done a bit differently in De Wallen. I wonder if the killer was counting on it. The constant hustle and bustle, the tourist hubs, the lackadaisical cops—might be more difficult to find this guy than we first thought."

"Don't give up hope yet. This Mr. Osloo sounds like a prime candidate."

Adele muttered, "Let's just hope the dog didn't eat Jansen's police report."

CHAPTER NINE

Settling in their borrowed vehicle, which Foucault had set up with the station, Adele scowled at the police report they'd been provided. Ink was stained, smudged. The whole thing was in Dutch. A big red circle around the address was the only reason they'd even managed to plug the coordinates into the GPS.

Now, Adele sighed as John maneuvered them through the streets of Amsterdam.

"Looks like he's just outside De Wallen," John said, studying the small purple line on their GPS. Even the instructions had been in Dutch until John had figured out, with much cursing and fury, how to change the settings.

They were leaving behind the interconnecting network of shops, brothels, and old canals lined by rows of metal bollards and old-school bars.

"There we are," John said suddenly, pointing as the GPS chirped their arrival. "There's a light on—Mr. Osloo is home."

Adele and John both tensed as Renee pulled their car along the curb outside the single-story house. Feet hit the pavement lightly, doors shut quietly, the two of them moved with careful motions towards the house.

Adele peered through the front window, orange light beaming out into the shadows of the late afternoon. Curtains cut off the view from inside the house. A small white door-cam centered the wooden frame. The two agents took the sturdy wooden steps, reaching the front door where John knocked loudly.

"Interpol!" he called.

Adele tried the bell but heard no ring. "Disconnected, I think," she muttered.

John nodded. Knocked louder again. "Interpol!" he said, raising the volume of his voice as well.

They waited awkwardly, standing on the porch. But there was no response.

John tried the door, but it didn't budge. "Locked," he said.

Adele frowned, side-stepping a deck chair and peering through the bright, front window. She had to press her cheek against the cool glass, her breath fogging the surface as she tried to catch a glance past the edge of the curtain.

"Anything?" John's voice rumbled along with another echoing knock.

Adele began to shake her head, her hair shifting next to her cheek, but then she went still. Through, the curtain, along the edge of the window, she spotted a silhouette standing in the living room. Prickles erupted up her spine, and she nearly withdrew, but something about the silhouette caused her to peer closer.

She strained, one eye closed, face still against the glass.

The figure in the middle of the room was motionless... standing on a chair. The man's head was bowed, his hands clasped in front of him as if in prayer. Suddenly, he crossed himself and looked sharply up. Bloodshot eyes peered towards where Adele was peeking. Those eyes widened in horror, and Adele suddenly realized what she was witnessing.

"John—break the door!" she shouted, lurching back and slamming a hand against the glass. "Don't!" she screamed. "Don't do it!"

John didn't need a second invitation, likely heeding the urgency in Adele's voice. His large foot carried the full weight of his massive frame careening into the door. A splintering sound. Then another sound from the house. Sobbing. Heavy, wailing.

"Please go away!" the voice shouted.

"Mr. Osloo—get off that chair! Don't move!" Adele shouted. Really, she just hoped to keep him in conversation.

John lurched back, aimed, and tried again. Another *thump* of his foot against the door. Another loud splintering *crack*! And this time the door caved in completely.

Adele hurtled the broken wooden frame. The top half dangled on a brass hinge. John kicked the rest free and followed after.

Adele had been right in her guess. The scene confronting her set her teeth on edge. Mr. Osloo was hanging himself, standing on a rickety chair, a thick rope around his neck, the other end looped over an exposed ceiling joist. Tears streamed down thick cheeks, bunched up from the pressure and gathered blood.

"Don't!" she tried to shout, but too late.

Mr. Osloo kicked the chair with his heel, desperate. The wooden frame clattered to the ground. A long moaning sound was cut suddenly short, replaced by huffing breaths and deep gurgling. Adele lunged towards the man, his legs kicking wildly, his hands scrambling at the thick rope digging into his thorax.

"John!" she screamed. "Help me! Renee!" She tried to speak further but caught a boot to the chin. She tasted blood but didn't retreat, holding her arms up to block the kicks and latching onto the man's legs, trying to heave him up.

Her shoulders strained and her heart hammered.

John Renee thundered towards her, and a second later her burden became much lighter as Renee lifted the man bodily, placing him on his shoulders.

"Not today!" Renee snapped.

Adele pulled her utility knife from her belt. "Hold him!" she called.

The man was spluttering, gasping, and weeping now. He tried to shake his head, but it just rubbed his flesh raw against the rope. Adele hurtled on top of the dining room table, clambering to the edge. She extended the knife and began sawing at the rope.

Mr. Osloo's arms went limp, his eyes bulging in his face like a frog's. Tears streamed along his cheeks, and he held Adele's gaze, a pleading look in his eyes.

"P-please," he choked. "Please just leave."

"I'm sorry," Adele murmured and she truly meant it. "I can't do that. I'm sorry sir." She sawed the rope as John held the man aloft. Bits of fiber tickled her fingers, trickling like sawdust as she worried the strands.

And then, it snapped, and the man let out a wheezing gasp, collapsing on top of Agent Renee. The two hit the ground in a pile, both letting out whooshing sounds as air fled their lungs. Mr. Osloo rolled off, his back shaking, his arms trembling. His fingers scrabbled at his throat, trying to pull the rope free.

Adele dropped to his side, her hand half reaching for her cuffs, but then wandering to the small of the fellow's back. "Sir," she said, concern in her tone. "Sir are you alright?"

He collapsed on the ground while John simultaneously surged to his feet. Renee kept a hand braced against Adele's shoulder as if preparing to yank her back at a moment's notice. His other hand snaked his phone from his pocket, and Adele listened as he called for paramedics.

But most her attention fixated on their suspect. Mr. Osloo turned slowly, collapsing against the toppled chair, using the backrest to support himself. The rope still hung about his throat like a tie, and his fingers touched at his neck as he hissed and wheezed. His voice came warbled, restrained. "Just shoot me," he whispered, tears still streaming. "Please, just kill me..."

Adele's expression flickered into a frown; she remained crouched next to him, looking the man in the eye. "Sir, paramedics are on their way. You're going to be fine. But I need to talk to you for a second. Can you speak to me, sir?"

He looked at her and let out a shaking sigh. "Did the neighbors call you?" he asked.

Adele paused, but then realized what he meant and shook her head. "No, sir. I'm not here about... about this. Or, at least, I wasn't. I wanted to speak to you about the incident at the Carmine's Offer brothel in De Wallen."

The man flinched, and an intense look of shame crossed his features. He leaned back, wheezing at the ceiling where the rest of the frayed rope still dangled.

"Not my proudest moment," he whispered. "She just looked so much like her." His eyes fell, descending to a portrait on the wall above the table. The portrait's glass had been smashed.

In it, a smiling man she barely recognized as the fellow on the floor stood next to a beaming woman. The sun shone behind them, and they stood next to a broad lake. There was something so tranquil, so peaceful about the image.

Nothing like the scene they'd stumbled on here.

Adele noticed the woman in the picture had blonde hair. "Who is that, sir?" she said.

"M-my wife," he wheezed. "You should've just let me die. Why didn't you let me die?" He screamed this now, spittle flying. Adele stood slowly, wiping at her cheek.

"Where is your wife now, sir?" Adele asked.

His mouth opened, his breath coming in a gasp. A strand of saliva stretched along his lips as he shuddered, trying to speak but unable to find the words. At last, with a sob, he whispered, "Dead. Six months ago. I shouldn't have gone to see those whores... but she just looked so much like Katarin. I—just wanted to be near her. Just for a bit longer." He shoulders shook horribly.

"The prostitute looked like your wife?"

He didn't reply. She wasn't sure he'd even heard the question. He was staring at the photograph on the wall once more.

"I can't imagine what she'd think of me now," he whispered. He doubled over, holding his head in his hands. In the background, Adele listened as Renee directed the paramedics to them.

She let out a faint sigh, staring down at the grieving man. This was often the hardest part, pushing aside her sense of compassion in order to reach a conclusion. The man was clearly distraught, but that didn't mean he wasn't a killer.

"These women," she pressed a bit harder, "the ones you visited at night—they resemble your wife."

The man just nodded, fingers digging deep grooves into his tear-streaked cheeks. "I just wanted to hold her again," he whispered. "Just hold her. I don't know what to do without her."

"Sir," Adele said, "I have to know, where were you Tuesday night?"

He looked up at last, his eyes wet. "I—I what?"

"Tuesday night, sir," she said, as gently as she could manage. "Where were you?"

"Umm... Tuesday? Just... I..." He blinked as if confused for a moment, but then waved a hand off to the side towards a calendar dangling from the small, wooden handle of a cupboard. "Group," he said. "Tuesdays are group."

Adele kept an eye on the grieving man and moved in the direction of the indicated calendar. There, she spotted a neat, organized schedule laid out. Each Tuesday was circled with red. And the time slot of 7:30-10:30 was written on each one.

"John," Adele murmured, "what time was our suspect on the camera at Red Letter?"

John lowered his phone, frowned, then said, "10:00, why?"

Adele sighed, giving a faint shake of her head. She turned back to Mr. Osloo. "Is there anyone who can verify your whereabouts?" she said.

The crying man wiped at his face with the back of his sleeve, looking confused now. For a man who'd just tried to take his life, it was odd to see a slow sense of self-preservation descend. "I—I didn't do anything..." he said slowly. "Is this about the prostitutes? I haven't been back since... well, since then... I swear!"

"What is this group?" she asked, tapping the calendar.

"Grief counseling," he said. "I can give you the number of the organizer. She can vouch for me. I was there on Tuesday. What is this about?"

Adele sighed. As she'd thought. This wasn't their man. Of course, they'd have to follow up the claim and speak to this counselor. But the man didn't fit the bill. For one, now that he was sitting upright, his shoulders were too narrow to be those of the man she'd seen in the video footage.

She sighed, glancing towards the frayed rope above the toppled chair. "We need that number, sir," she said simply.

In the distance, she heard the sound of approaching sirens. They'd saved a life tonight. She glanced towards Mr. Osloo, feeling another pang of pity. The hospital would keep an eye on him, along with an officer. That would give them enough time to check the alibi.

But as Adele looked at the grieving man, all she felt was sadness. He hadn't tried to hurt her, to fight them. He'd tried to hurt himself. They'd saved a life tonight.

But the killer was still at large, and others were still in danger.

CHAPTER TEN

The weight of night descended on Adele's shoulders, draping like a cape. De Wallen looked different at night: the canals and old waterways, hinting at the bygone medieval city center, connected cramped alleys illuminated in bright glows from the various brothels and old-fashioned bars lining the waterways and sidewalks. It verged on the beautiful and the perverse. She walked alongside John—again the designated caller. She waited, listening faintly in the cool night, strolling along the boardwalk as Renee became agitated.

"It's a simple question," John was saying. "Was Mr. Osloo there the *entire* night?" He waited, rolling his eyes as well as his forefinger as if to say *get on with it.*

Adele hid a smile as she walked alongside her partner. Perhaps it was the cool breeze, or simply the atmosphere, but after a quick glance over her shoulder, she leaned in, slipping her elbow through John's.

John winked at her as they strolled, but just as quickly frowned. "Yes—Interpol, ma'am. Like I said. It's an ongoing investigation, I can't tell you." John paused, then let out a long sigh. "That's all I wanted to know. Ten-thirty? You're sure? A local officer is going to come by tomorrow to get a statement. Where can he best find you?"

After hammering out some final details, John hung up with a long sigh, tilting his head to stare at the dark sky. "Lord help us."

Adele sniffed. "Not sure he's around these parts." She frowned towards a window where a pretty, plus-sized woman was entrancing a row of youngsters gathered by the glass. A few of the onlookers didn't look like they'd made it out of high school yet.

Adele looked away, her arm still looped through John's. "Mr. Osloo's alibi?"

"Tentatively confirmed. One of the locals has to take her statement. But no dice on Osloo."

Adele bit her lower lip, holding back a foul word. Not that this surprised her. She'd already written Mr. Osloo off as an unlikely candidate. But what did that mean for their next move? The Dutch police had already put out a warning to all the brothels in the Red Light District, specifically warning them about blonde women that fit the description of the killer's victims.

"Call it a night?" John asked, swinging his elbow and causing Adele's to swish back and forth as well. Sometimes the big man acted like a schoolboy, but there was no one who made her feel safer when wandering dark streets in foreign city.

"Maybe..." she paused in the middle of the street, glancing up and down the boulevard. Crowds had dwindled, tourists still lingered but moved quicker from location to location. De Wallen had served the killer well so far. "He struck twice in three days," Adele said quietly. "Means he might be on the prowl tonight."

She looked down the street in the other direction, looking as the young men watching the large woman made gestures at the prostitute.

She turned back to John. "What if we stroll around a bit?" she said with a shrug. "John—hey *John.*"

He blinked, ripping his gaze away from another model in a window on the opposite side of the street. "Yes?" he said quickly. "I'm—umm, what?"

Adele rolled her eyes, yanking John roughly by the elbow and leading him up the street, along the sidewalk. She wasn't quite sure what she expected to find out here in the night. Already, a thick cover of darkness would obscure the less-than-reputable sorts.

But De Wallen wasn't *that* large. The culture here was so different from anywhere she'd been before; she was still trying to get her bearings.

"Look at that," John muttered, pointing. The St. Nicolas Basilica's turrets jutted in the night sky, near enough to windows with scantily clad women to strike an odd juxtaposition.

Adele kept tugging insistently at his arm, moving along the streets. A busker crooned softly where he sat perched on a park bench. A few other shops boasted late night service with sex shops located next to Middle-Eastern restaurants.

Adele noted a tall man following a younger woman. She went stiff, staring as the two left a café. But a second later, the man caught up with the woman, and she leaned against him giggling and planting a kiss on his cheek.

Adele sighed, looking away.

"You know," John said carefully, "you're prettier than all of these women."

"Thank you, Renee," Adele said with a snort, patting him on the back of the hand.

"And," John began slowly, "coming to a new place like this... a new city? Might be nice to explore new things."

Adele's eyes narrowed and she only afforded Renee a faint "mhmm."

"I mean, *some* of these women are quite interesting, no? Not that I'm looking. Of course not. Never."

"Of course."

"Just... you know, if *you* were feeling... experimental..."

Adele turned, looking John dead in the eyes. "A threesome? Really?"

"What? I never—I didn't say—"

"Sure," Adele said without batting an eyelid. "I'm game."

John's mouth half unhinged. "I-I... you are?"

"As long as I get to choose the third."

"Wonderful—yes, of course, of course!"

Adele tapped her chin with a finger, pretending to be lost in thought. "Honestly, John, I'm impressed by your willingness to try new things."

"Thank you," he said with a nod and a sniff. "I do pride myself on being open-minded."

"I'm thinking... tall. Muscles. Definitely. I don't *mind* facial hair. But he has to be well-groomed. What do you think?"

John gaped at her, blinked, swallowed. "I—*he* has to be?"

Adele kept her expression solemn, though inwardly she felt a wicked, mischievous jolt of delight at his gob smacked expression. "Yes, of course. Like you said, I get to choose our partner. Thank you, John—very, very considerate of you." She patted him on the arm again.

"W-I didn't... but—Adele..." John stumbled over his words, spluttering as he moved alongside her. "You know what... Maybe it's not such a good idea. I wouldn't want to make you uncomfortable."

"I'm perfectly comfortable John."

It took him a second to notice the faint curve of her lips. Then, his eyes narrowed. "You're teasing me..."

Adele smirked, displaying a Cheshire grin. "I don't know, am I?" But as she said it, she trailed off, her eyes darting towards a well-lit window across from a café.

A blonde woman was dancing in the window, swaying in time with some unheard music. Long, fake eyelashes fluttered along with the crook of a finger as she beckoned towards Adele and John. But Adele's gaze flitted from the woman towards the man in the alley across the street.

He wasn't like the other tourists. He wasn't pretending not to watch, but he also wasn't up against the glass, ogling. Rather, he stood across the street, in the folds of an alley's shadows, watching the blonde woman.

He wore a newsboy cap angled low over his eyes, his hands jammed in his pockets. When he caught Adele watching him, he pushed off the wall suddenly and began to move quickly up the street, in the opposite direction of the agents.

"John..." Adele murmured.

"It was just a joke, Adele. Yes. I was just joking. I don't—I'm not actually—"

"John! Look. That man, see him?"

John's flustered prattle trailed off. He followed Adele's indicating finger and gave a nod. The two agents hesitated, poised on the sidewalk both peering in the direction of the retreating man. The man in the cap shot a quick look over his shoulder.

Adele glanced away, pretending she'd been admiring the blonde woman in the window as well. "Is he still looking?" Adele whispered.

John grunted. "Turned off down a street. What's wrong?"

"I—he was watching her..." Adele whispered, pointing towards the woman in the window. "Plus... just something off. He was in the alley."

John nodded slowly and then, his arm still hooked in Adele's, he began to move with long, rolling steps up the street towards the intersection where the man in the cap had disappeared. Adele moved twice as fast to keep up with her partner.

"Careful," she whispered. "Don't spook him. Not yet."

The two of them slowed but kept moving as quickly as possible towards the edge of the café. Then, they rounded onto the intersecting street in pursuit of the strange man.

CHAPTER ELEVEN

The man had paused again, peering through another brothel's window. Adele and John kept their distance as they slowly followed the man up the street. This had been his second stop in as many minutes, and again, as Adele watched him from where she lingered near a bus-stop, the man's face creased in a sudden bout of rage.

He glared at the woman in the window, his lip curling into a sneer. And again, as he had before, he turned away in disgust, trudging off and muttering darkly beneath his breath.

"Someone's not in a good mood," John murmured.

Adele didn't say anything, still maintaining a sufficient gap as they followed the man through the district. He paused near another display window and again cursed, slamming a fist into his hand. This time, he even flashed the bird at the woman in the window and spat.

Adele blinked in surprise as spittle flecked the glass. The woman shouted something from inside her protective cage, returning the middle finger. But the man threw his hand up in disgust and dismissal and trudged to the end of the street, turning down it and disappearing behind the side of the nearest brothel.

Adele and John picked up their pace, hurrying to the edge of the street. Adele turned to follow, her reflection chasing her along the many glass windows.

But she suddenly pulled to a halt. Her eyes darted up and down the new street. "Where'd he go?" she said suddenly.

John came to a halt at her side as well, running a hand through his dark hair as he huffed. "Shit... Think he saw us?"

Adele winced, but then frowned. "Unless... unless he saw what he was looking for," she murmured. She pointed first to one side of the street, then to the next. Two brothels, both facing each other, both with scantily clad women in the window. Perhaps it was just Adele's imagination, but these women seemed to be moving a bit more zealously than previous dancers. Perhaps out of the competition factor of each other—both had a perfect view of one another across the street.

Such a strange place. But Adele wasn't here for the hefty dose of culture shock. She cursed, pointing off to the right. "You take the brunette!" she ordered. "I've got the redhead."

John blinked, gaping after her.

"The brothel, John!" she snapped. "Look for him—hurry!"

John's mouth closed and he gave a quick nod. He picked up the pace, jogging towards the indicated brothel while Adele hastened across the street.

She paused in the door, once again glancing up and down the street. No sign of the angry man in the hat. Had he hidden down an alley? Had he given them the slip?

She seethed but shook her head. The man had seemed so determined, looking for... for something... someone?

She cursed, pushing elbow first through the swinging glass door, small, speckled fairy lights illuminating her sleeve. She didn't trust the germs on the door handle. As she shouldered through, a big man, built uncomfortably like her father, was standing behind a desk. The man was about the Sergeant's age, had a similar beer belly and strong forearms. Thank heavens he wasn't also wearing a t-shirt with soup stains; Adele wasn't sure her subconscious could've taken it.

Even still, she felt completely uncomfortable standing in front of the bouncer. She wondered what her father might say if he ever saw her in such a place.

Even this consideration, the notion of her old man in a place like this, caused her stomach to churn. Some things were best left deep, deep in the imagination, hidden from the light of thought.

"Umm, sorry," she stuttered, "I'm looking for a man. Did he come in here?"

The bouncer's eyes narrowed, and he gave a faint shake of his head. "No man," he muttered.

Adele sighed, ripping her badge from her pocket and flashing it. "Interpol," she said. "Please, I'm investigating an active case."

The bouncer glared at her, crossing his arms. Even the hair along his forearms looked like her father's. Shit. This whole place seemed designed to screw with her mind. Adele decided the next best option was to ignore the man completely. She tried to sidestep him, but he stepped as well.

Muscled and big though he was, he didn't touch her. At least the badge had earned that much.

"No man," the bouncer repeated.

"Two words at a time," she muttered. "I'm proud of you." As she spoke, she tried to peer past the fellow's ample waist, down the hall. She thought she spotted movement on the other side of a dangling, beaded curtain like the fringe of a weeping willow.

"No man!" he insisted, a bit more loudly, moving like a basketball player to block her progress without using his hands.

"Touch me," she said firmly, "and I'm going to take out some childhood anger, got it?" A part of her felt a strange, vindictive delight at the thought of burying her knee into the big man's belly.

Perhaps her daddy issues weren't as settled as she'd hoped. Still... she didn't hit him right away. That was some progress, wasn't it?

As she tried to sidestep the bouncer, someone suddenly screamed from down the hall.

Adele's eyes widened, the bouncer's followed, after a second, a bit slower on the uptake.

"Sorry," she said. "That's my cue." She shoved him, hard, leaning into it, and used the motion to sidestep, rushing down the hall.

"John!" She shouted over her shoulder, though she doubted he'd hear from across the street.

More shouting from down the hall, followed by loud, angry voices. The door at the far end was still open, where Adele had spotted motion. Now, though, a figure in a flat cap was stumbling into the hall, angrily yanking and jerking at the arm of a woman.

More shouting in Dutch. Adele wasn't sure what was being said but could tell by the enraged expressions on both the man and the prostitute that it wasn't anything nice.

The bouncer, seemingly deciding the real threat wasn't the cop, hurried behind Adele, rushing down the hall as well. The bouncer bumped into Adele, but then flung himself into a lurching grasp.

The man in the cap stopped mid-shout. He turned, eyes widening beneath his cap. And the bouncer slammed into him, bringing both of them down in a loud *thump!*

The girl stared down, horrified, her mouth forming a circle, and then she screamed, beating at the bouncer with a small, black purse with a golden clasp.

The man on the ground was protesting, kicking. The bouncer's head lifted, a grim look of satisfaction across his features. He posed almost heroically on top of the man he tackled. But the look of heroism only lasted until the black purse struck him on the nose.

"No!" the prostitute was shouting. She continued yelling, beating at the bouncer.

He blinked, raising a hand to protect his face and then deciding this new threat, armed with a purse, was a priority, he shoved off the man he'd tackled and grabbed the woman's wrist, restraining her.

Adele already had cuffs in her hand and dropped to her knee by the side of the man in the cap who pushed up, blinking blearily, and shaking his head, muttering beneath his breath. Sweat trickled down his face. He had features like a banker beneath the cap. Neat hair, glasses, and silver sideburns. The red flush, the sweat, and the wheezing sound he made as he rubbed his ribs somewhat ruined the "distinguished" look he was going for.

Adele pulled at the man, twisting at his arm, clicking the cuffs into place as she dragged him to his feet.

She heard the loud sound of thumping footsteps and the voice of John Renee behind her. "Adele! Are you okay!"

"Fine," she gasped, clicking the cuffs completely into place and then pulling at the man's collar to lead him away from where the woman was still trying to bludgeon the bouncer. "I think he might need some help," she said, breathing heavily.

John gave one look at the purse-wielding woman. He clicked his tongue. "She a suspect?"

Adele shook her head.

"Then I think he's got it handled," John said, wincing as the golden clasp of the purse struck the bouncer's nose again.

Adele rolled her eyes. "John..." she said.

"Fine," he muttered. And the big Frenchman marched towards the purse-wielding hooker to intervene.

CHAPTER TWELVE

He twisted the plastic straw, stirring it through the glass and trying to pick out the pleasant tinkle of ice against glass over the noise of the club. How people abided places like this never much made sense to him. Too much noise. Too much body heat. Sweat, drugs, drink... And inevitably the odor of vomit and urine in the bathrooms where the charming denizens missed their targets.

Still... he'd been patient.

And now his patience was rewarded.

There she was, pushing through one of the back doors now, coming from upstairs. A man accompanied her, smiling profusely and patting her arm. The tall woman smiled politely, gave the man a final kiss on the cheek, and then sent him off with a little push. The man was reluctant to leave, but with a heavy sigh finally retreated, moving away from the leggy woman.

She glanced around the room, adjusting her dress and tapping a finger to an ear to disentangle one of her earrings. Her eyes flitted towards where the man sat, his hand still resting on his glass of ice water.

As she looked his way, his heart hammered, and he forced a smile and a little wave. She noticed the motion of his hand and returned the smile and began strolling in his direction.

The man cleared his throat, quickly dabbing a napkin across his forehead, making sure to wipe the sweat free. He pushed to his feet, doing everything he could not to look in the direction of the other man who'd descended the stairs with his love.

A white-hot bolt of rage jolted through him. Even that little kiss, the faint push... All reminders of what the two of them had likely been doing upstairs. The FKK clubs weren't like normal dance clubs. They came with perks attached.

One such perk was strolling towards him as if she had all the time in the world and was making her way down a catwalk. She looked as good as he remembered her. Clear skin, sky blue eyes, blonde hair, smooth legs for days.

As he straightened, he adjusted his glasses, smiling nervously.

He moved around the table, approaching her as she neared. Ten feet. Five... He blinked, feeling a sudden jolt. Three. Two. They stood within a foot of each other. She was still smiling, but his own expression had slipped.

A faint flicker of horror twisted his stomach.

"No... no, no..." he whispered beneath his breath.

"Pardon me?" she asked, leaning in and placing a delicate hand to her ear so she could hear over the noise. Her earring, a little diamond heart, swished.

"You're—you're not who I thought you were," he said, his voice strained. She looked so similar. He'd done his research, hadn't he? A Belgian girl, just like him. He *knew* she'd been—but no. No, standing there, staring at her, he'd made a mistake.

How hard was it going to be to find her? How many more hours, days, weeks?

He let out a weary sigh, turning to leave.

But her fingers trailed against his arm. She leaned in close, and he felt the warmth of her body radiating against his skin. "Let me help you," she whispered in his ear. "I can be whoever you'd like me to be."

He turned back, staring at her. Those eyes... so familiar yet so different. Why did she have to be such a tease? Why did they all?

A pretense... a con. They were trying to play with his heart.

He felt his blood boiling again. That same rage from earlier returned, faster now. But he kept his expression impassive, his eyes blinking behind his spectacles. He cleared his throat and forced a polite smile.

"I'm sorry for wasting your time," he said.

Now she held his arm, though, her grip strong but comforting. She rubbed her hand up and down his arm. "It's not a waste. And my time is very affordable. Would you like to come see?"

The rage kept mounting. She wasn't who he'd come looking for. Just another fake. A copy—a counterfeit. And now here she was trying to pass off for someone she wasn't. He couldn't stand the deception. What sort of fool did she take him for!

His lips curled in a snarl, but he caught the gesture and coughed. "I—perhaps a few minutes of your time..."

"I'm afraid, my dear, it's by the hour. But I know you can afford it. You're not a loser, are you?"

His heart twisted in his chest. He wanted to reach out now to grab her by that beautiful, sloping neck. But no... not here. She wanted to play with him? He could play. She thought she could pretend to be someone she wasn't?

He could do the same.

Clearly, she thought he was an idiot. A fool. A weak little beta male. And so he coughed delicately, adjusted his glasses and stammered. "I—sorry," he said. "Sure. Great. An hour is fine. Where—I mean, oh my, this isn't normal for me, I assure you."

Her fingers trailed along his arm, tickling the inside of his palm. "Nor for me," she whispered. "Come, I'll show you my room."

He allowed her to guide him towards the base of the stairs. A large man in a tailored suit unhooked a velvet rope, allowing them to pass. He spotted the metal detector as they took the stairs and also the security camera above the entrance. The detector was no problem, but the camera caused him to duck his head and rub at his sleeves.

"Don't be nervous," she said with a playful giggle, still tugging him along.

He just nodded, allowing her to assume he was nervous. It had always amused him to let others underestimate him, ever since he'd been a child. People often looked right through him as if he were only so much upholstery. Not that this bothered him. It was his single greatest advantage.

And now, the bouncers didn't even cast him a second look.

He allowed the blonde woman with the blue eyes to guide him up red, velvet stairs, towards a curving hallway.

"My room is just this way," she said. "There's a shower. Would you like to start there?"

He didn't speak as she pushed open an oak door that smelled of varnish. The room itself was neat, clean. Either cleaners had been through since the last customer, or this was a different room than the one she'd just returned from.

"I'm going to take a quick shower," she said as she pushed the door shut. "Come join me if you'd like."

"I don't really want to get undressed," he said his voice timid. Inwardly, all he could really feel was rage. But it was easier to catch flies with honey. And so he ducked his head, shifting uncomfortably, dipping his shoulders in a sort of slouch.

An easy persona to adopt. Shy, coy, delicate. The sorts of things people saw when they looked at him. They just never looked closely enough.

The prostitute gave a clear little laugh like a bell. "I see," she said. "A cuddler, then? Well, in that case, would you like the bed or the couch?"

He glanced from one to the other, then gave a shrug of indifference.

"You don't happen to mind a little bit of light choking, do you?" he said.

This was blunt, and more straightforward than he was accustomed to, but his temper was burning hot. He could feel his anger ready to burst at the seams. She'd tried to trick him.

"Are you even Belgian?" he asked suddenly, his voice harsh.

She looked at him, startled. His expression returned to a docile, demure one just as quickly. She blinked, staring and then, like they always did, seemed to decide she'd mistaken his tone. "Belgian?" she said. "How did you know I was Belgian?"

"Oh, I guess I heard it somewhere."

"Did another client send you? Who? They're entitled to a week of discounts."

"No, nothing like that. Just... I thought maybe you were using a fake name. When I saw you—I thought you were someone else."

"A fake name? I haven't told you my name."

He let out a little puff of air and glanced off, reorienting. "No, no I guess you haven't. But about my request?"

"The choking?" She frowned now, one hand on her hip. "I thought you were a nice little man. No, no choking. I don't do BDSM. There are other girls for that."

"Right, *other* girls," he said, his teeth grinding. He was no longer looking down, no longer looking off. He stared through his glasses, his eyes fixed on her beautiful face.

A fake face. A fake woman.

"I'd like you to reconsider," he said, his lips tight. "I won't be too harsh. Just a little."

She frowned now, shaking her head. "No, sir. No choking. You know what, this isn't worth my time. Thank you, but I don't think this is going to work."

She moved away from the bathroom entrance towards the door again. He stepped aside, pretending like he was going to let her pass.

Anyone else, she might have looked back. A thickset man with muscles, a douchebag with an attitude—any of it might have warranted a second glance.

But he was forgettable. She didn't even glance at him as she reached for the door handle.

He pulled the silk scarf from his pocket, wrapping it around his hand as she began to open the door. "I don't like being told no," he murmured. "It feels like rejection. Hell, that's why I'm here in the first place."

Now she did pause, did begin to turn, her beautiful features creased into a frown. The door was only ajar, her fingers still resting on the handle.

"What was that?"

He met her gaze, those beautiful blue eyes. Now that he saw her, up close, he couldn't believe how stupid he'd been. Of course it wasn't *her.* How could this cow be his beloved? This was just a wretched little flesh suit.

"Bitch..." he whispered.

"Excuse me?" she said, frowning now. "That's it. I'm getting security."

She flung the door open, and he kicked it shut. The door slammed, she tried to scream, but his hands darted forward, the silk scarf wrapped tight. He was fast—very fast. A lean, athletic build beneath the docile posture.

Now her eyes bugged in fear. The scarf wrapped around her neck, tight. The scream died in her throat. She tried to gasp, but it was too late for this.

He dragged her, hissing and grunting, yanking her towards the bed. Her fingers pulled at the scarf, but to no avail.

"Do you see me now?" he whispered in her ear, his muscles tensed. She tried to kick, to scream again. But this only cost her more precious air she couldn't spare.

He felt the slow, delightful release of rage leaving his body, through his hands, through his fingers. His stomach twisted; his skin prickled. A rush of endorphins, of chemical reward, as he twisted the scarf, tighter, tighter.

What lovely shades the human face displayed in the right conditions. All purple and pink and eventually, after some time, a pleasing gray.

CHAPTER THIRTEEN

Adele and John stood outside the brothel, still trying to separate the woman from the man in the cap. Every time they caught a look at the other, they burst into an argument, waving fingers and shaking fists despite their cuffs.

Adele sighed, weathering another storm of diatribe before raising her voice. "Enough!" she said.

The street was mostly empty. The prostitute in the window across the way wasn't dancing now, but instead watched the scene curiously, wrapping a see-through shawl over her bare shoulders. Adele tried to move to block the line of sight from the man with the cap. Now, though, his only glances of ire were reserved for the woman in Renee's cuffs.

One thing stood out to Adele: the woman didn't match the killer's type. She was petite, brunette. And now the first to speak in English. "He's a fool!" she declared, pointing angrily at the man. "An idiot!"

The man shook his head, looking at Adele beseechingly. "It isn't good," he said in a much heavier accent. "She's demeaning herself." Louder, he called past Adele. "Demeaning!"

"You are demeaning!" she yelled back.

John sighed, trying to stand between the two of them. Adele waited patiently for this newest outburst to die down. Then, she said, "Do you know this man?"

The woman snorted, muttering something beneath her breath.

"What was that?" Adele insisted.

She muttered a few more choice insults in Dutch but then ended in English. "Pig-headed brother."

"Imagine if our father could see you like this!" he yelled back, rattling his cuffs, his hands clasped as if pleading. "He'd turn in his grave!"

"You dare!" she squealed, scandalized. "You bring up papa! Heartless, pig-headed brother."

"Slutty, fool-hearted floozy of a sister!" he retorted back.

"Sibling squabble," John said with a shrug.

Adele rubbed a hand over her face.

"Are you telling me you two are brother and sister?" she asked.

For the first time, this question earned her a few moments of peace. The two siblings glanced between each other, then at her. "What else would we be?" the man said, slowly.

Then, his eyes widened in horror. "Yuck!" he yelled.

"Gross!" she said.

"Disgusting," they echoed together, in nearly identical intonations.

"Siblings," John said with a confirming nod.

The man stammered. "I—I didn't mean to cause a scene, officer."

"Agent," Adele corrected glumly.

He didn't notice. "I just came to bring her home! She's bringing shame to our family. Look at her! Look at what she's wearing!"

"Weirdo," the sister retorted. "Stop staring."

"I'm not staring!" he snapped. "I feel ready to vomit!"

Adele leaned over, slowly wrangling the man's waving hands, unlocking the cuffs. It took him a second to realize what she was doing and go still. He blinked in surprise. Adele glanced towards the woman and waved at John, who also began to uncuff her. "I'm guessing you don't agree with your brother's assessment?" Adele said faintly.

The woman snorted, shaking her head, her dark curls bouncing. "It is legal what I do. It should be legal. Everywhere! I will not let him shame me! Not again—not like always!"

"Always, hah! You've been a rebel for decades."

"You've been a meddler for just as long!"

Adele felt her ears ringing and wanted nothing more than to jam her fingers in them and cut off the incessant noise. Instead, she calmed herself and pointed towards the man. "You can't drag your sister away if she doesn't want to go. I'm going to let you loose, but you can't come back here, understand?"

The man scowled at Adele, then his sister, but finally, with a wrinkled nose, he nodded once.

"And you," Adele said, pointing towards the woman. "Inside voice, I'm begging you."

The cuffs were now removed, and the siblings shot each other angry glances. The woman said, "I can go?"

John raised an eyebrow at Adele, but she just nodded.

The man took this as his cue also. He tipped his hat low and, muttering darkly, stomped away. The woman yelled something after him and pushed into the brothel once more. The fairy lights flashed as the door slowly swung, and the man in the cap turned up the end of the road, stomping like a petulant child.

And once again, Adele and John were left in the dark streets of De

Wallen.

"Well, there goes that," she said, rubbing at the bridge of her noise.

John wriggled a knuckle in his ear. "What was that?" he said playfully. "I think I lost my hearing."

Adele smirked, knuckling John's shoulder. He leaned in and gave her a quick side hug. Still leaning close, his head against hers, he said, "Care to call it a night?"

"I guess so. It's not like we have a lead..." Adele bunched her hand in frustration at this admission.

She glanced towards the darkened sky, trying to pick out sparse starlight amidst the canopy of black, but the lights from the brothels and city streets veiled the celestial. She liked to keep her feet planted firmly on the ground anyhow. She slipped her arm from John, rubbing her hands. "Scope out a hotel yet?" she asked.

John smirked. "Found one—work comped for the room."

"One room?" she said, feeling a flicker of unease. "On a *work* trip? You know Foucault checks the pay stubs, right?"

"Oh, please—Adele he already knows we're together."

"I don't think he does. If he did, we wouldn't still be partnered. You know how he is with that sort of thing."

John snorted dismissively already moving back up the street. "If you want to book another room, be my guest!" he called over his shoulder. "I wasn't looking forward to our ménage à trois with your hairy hunk anyway."

"Muscled, too!" Adele admonished, hiding a smirk and picking up the pace to catch her partner.

John wasn't wrong. A good night's rest might give them a new perspective come morning. The killer was still out there, and he wasn't done. Men like this didn't stop unless someone did it for them.

She didn't look to the left or the right as she hastened down the street after Renee, but as she picked up her pace, her phone suddenly began to buzz.

Adele flinched and realized another ring-tone was coming from John's phone as well. As if they'd practiced the synchronization, both of them lifted their phones simultaneously and said, "Yes?"

Adele listened to the gruff tone of Agent Foucault. For a minute, her stomach fell. Was he calling about the individually booked room? Shit—John never did know how to be careful. She hated the thought of being separated and paired with different partners. But Foucault was a stickler for that sort of thing.

"Agent Sharp?" Foucault said. "Where are you and Renee?"

"I—in De Wallen, sir."

"Did Paige reach John?"

Adele glanced towards her boyfriend who was frowning as he listened to his own device. "Looks like it, yes."

"Well, pack your bags, Adele. Killer isn't in De Wallen anymore."

"What? Sorry, I mean excuse me, sir?"

"Another body, Agent Sharp. Another murder—a blonde prostitute at a nightclub. Strangled. She's in Germany."

Adele stared off down the street, her skin prickling. "G-Germany, sir? You're sure?"

Foucault didn't even reply to this, instead sighing wearily.

"Of course you're sure. We'll head there right away, sir. We'll be at the scene come morning."

"Good. And Agent Sharp, how are you doing?"

"I—excuse me?" She felt a flicker of fear. Why was he asking her that? Was it about John? Worse—was it about the painter? Icy tendrils of fear curled up her spine.

But Foucault just said, "The victims look like you, yes? You're still able to focus?"

"Oh—yes. Of course, sir. I'm fine. Thank you."

A grunt. Then he hung up.

John lowered his phone a few moments later. The two of them stared across at each other, lights flickering out of the corners of their eyes.

Adele couldn't lie to herself. She wasn't going to miss this place.

John looked somewhat disappointed. He shrugged. "Guess we're headed to Germany," he said.

Adele was already dialing a taxi.

CHAPTER FOURTEEN

All Adele heard was the tap of their footsteps against the tiled airport floors as she and John hastened out the glass doors, onto the curb. The airport was nearly empty—the sound of nighttime traffic a distant whir.

A single beige taxi, with its blinkers on, sat by the curb, and a yawning man in the front seat lowered the front window, peering towards them. "Sharp?" he called.

Adele flashed a thumbs up.

The ride passed quickly, moving through the deep night. The short flight from Amsterdam to just south of Dortmund had given Adele time to dwell on the case. Now, as their driver pushed the speed limit for the nighttime trip, she mulled over the case notes once more.

John was in the front seat. She didn't mind. He needed the leg room. Besides, sitting in the dark, in the back, gave her a sense of security. Isolation.

She vaguely remembered a dark park, low mist curling across the ground. Her stomach twisted, but she hissed, allowing the thought to lift.

What if they were approaching this wrong? The killer had seemed clever—avoiding the cameras, targeting women in a busy district where it would be impossible to narrow down on a single likely target. He had a type, that much was clear...

But what if this wasn't about avoiding law enforcement.

What if he wasn't being careful at all. Was he a reckless killer? He'd escaped detection though. So why travel to Germany? Already, reports were being run with DGSI and Interpol, cross-checking all flights to the Netherlands and to Germany with male passengers.

That list alone wouldn't be enough, but it would give another point of contact. Another clue in case he slipped up.

Partly cautious, but partly reckless. It didn't really make sense.

"Come on," Adele murmured beneath her breath. What explained this sudden shift? Why was he in Germany now? Why break the pattern...

Unless this wasn't about fulfilling some sadistic urge. What if killing wasn't the point at all? That might explain the whiplash of decision-making. Maybe he was cautious because he was a cautious man. But he was desperate as well.

Why desperate?

Why Germany?

Fear?

...Love?

Money?

She tapped her fingers against the windowsill. He wasn't robbing the prostitutes... What was he afraid of? How could love possibly factor into it?

She thought back to the man tugging at his sister's arm, trying to drag her from the brothel. Was she missing something as obvious as a familial relationship? Was the killer trying to save these women somehow?

She wrinkled her nose. None of it made sense.

"Club Apollo?" the driver suddenly said.

Adele looked up in surprise and blinked through the tinted glass of the beige German taxi to spot flashing red and blue lights all up and down one side of a street beneath a bright, flashing pink and azure sign that read *Apollo.*

"Know anything about this place?" John asked, glancing at the driver.

The man blushed, ducking his head and muttering a small prayer. "No, no," he said after. "No, no." He gave a flick of his fingers as if shooing the two agents.

They both obliged, slipping from the cab onto the concrete sidewalk in the dead of night, surrounded by German police outside a sex club.

The doors to the club were propped open by cinderblocks. Cops moved about on the steps, and a few BKA agents—judging by their suits—maneuvered inside the club. Otherwise, the place was vacant. "They let everyone go..." Adele murmured, taking the steps slowly. She flashed her ID to make passage between two plain-clothes officers.

"Mistake," John grunted. "They might have just let the bastard slip away."

Adele paused then shook her head. "I don't think it would have mattered," she murmured. "He would have been long gone."

"You sound certain."

"I am. He's cautious," she said, "But sporadically reckless." She looked around again at the familiar lettering on the side of the police cars. *Polizei.* "He came to Germany for Christ's sakes."

John just shrugged and moved up the stairs, past the cinderblocks and into the sex club. The scent of sweat still lingered on the air. A few of the strobing lights over the dance floor had been shut off. But one was still flashing, spinning and casting bright, white light in every direction.

Abandoned drinks adorned tables and counters. Adele spotted a forgotten purse near the bar, and a couple of jackets on a coat rack by the door.

"They must have cleared everyone in a hurry," she said. She was confident the killer had already made good his getaway; for all they knew he was already halfway across the country.

"Body still up there," John warned. "Think we should wait for paramedics?" A couple of BKA agents frowned as they passed by, but no one intercepted the two agents. John and Adele had worked with BKA in the past, and Adele recognized a few of the faces. She didn't doubt some of them knew her as well.

She gestured towards a stairwell with a velvet rope where more cops were stationed, standing in a circle and muttering to each other.

"Hello!" she called, raising a hand and speaking in German. "Interpol," she said. "Is the crime scene upstairs?" She pointed.

Two of the cops looked at her suspiciously. And older man with a thin, white mustache nodded once. "Top floor," he said, "Second door. Coroner is still in there, though. He's in a bad mood. Woke him late."

Adele nodded in gratitude at the warning but gestured for John to fall into step behind her. The two of them maneuvered up the stairs, the velvet carpeting softening their footsteps.

The door in question was easy to find. Thanks in part to the coroner assistants standing outside, and the dark mutterings coming from within.

"I'm not in the mood," John growled, stifling a yawn.

"Be nice," Adele whispered. "We're not here for trouble."

"Whatever."

The entered through the door, sidling past the assistants and facing the crime scene.

The body was still on the bed. Adele let out a faint sigh. She'd grown accustomed to seeing the victims as photographs. Facing the woman herself now made her unsettled.

Like the other women, this newest victim had been posed. Her arms at her side, her legs straight, neat. Her eyes stared lifelessly at the ceiling. If Adele hadn't known better, she might have simply thought the woman was taking a quick rest.

An older woman with a very heavy chest and an equally heavy

scowl was moving light on her feet about the prostitute's room, a small black satchel in one hand. The large woman leaned near the body, her gloved fingers touching the wrist. Then she muttered, shaking her head and examining the dead woman's eyes.

"Excuse me?" Adele called.

The woman ignored them, moving on to the victim's neck and then calling through the door. "Where's that damn stretcher?"

A couple of the assistants muttered back and forth and then one beat a hasty retreat down the stairs.

"Pardon," Adele said. "We're with Interpol."

The heavy-chested, older woman looked over, glaring. "Don't give a shit, do I?" she snapped. "Get out until I'm done."

John glanced at Adele, muttering in French. "What did she say?"

"Umm... hello."

"Liar."

Adele elbowed him, keeping her tone pleasant. "We just came from Amsterdam," she said. "We're working the case."

The woman perked up at this, exhaling heavily. In fact, she was breathing as if she'd just run a marathon, or as if she had a bout of asthma. She shook her head. "Don't know anything about Amsterdam. You sure you don't mean Belgium?"

"I—umm, why Belgium?" Adele asked, grateful for the moment that they weren't being shouted at.

"Because," the coroner said with a glare, "that's where the whore is from."

"She's Belgian?"

"Yes—her ID is on that dresser over there next to that wallet and purse. Now be quiet—I'm trying to focus. Who were you with again?"

"Interpol," Adele began to reply, but the woman across the room by the bed was no longer paying attention.

Adele glanced up at Renee. Quietly, so as to not disturb the coroner, she whispered, "Victim was Belgian..."

John frowned. "Wasn't the first victim also Belgian?" he said, also keeping his voice low.

Adele nodded, glancing back at the body on the bed. The similarities didn't end there, either. The blonde woman on the bed was also tall, also leggy. She also had the same sort of upturned nose and sharp cheekbones.

"Any idea of the murder weapon?" Adele asked, raising her voice again.

"Hell if I know," the large woman grunted. "You'll have my report like everyone else in the morning."

"Was it strangulation?"

"I said you'll have my—wait, what?"

"Strangulation," Adele insisted.

"It looks like it, but I can't be sure. No handprints. If she was choked to death, the killer used something. Ligature marks, see."

Adele peered in and nodded. A long, thin bruise, already having turned deep purple. "How long has she been dead?" Adele continued, polite yet indifferent to the coroner's bad mood. She'd worked with surly before.

John Renee was also peering at the corpse, a glower on his handsome features.

"Can't tell," the coroner said. "Not yet, at least. But I can tell you she put up a fight."

Adele's heart skipped. "She did? That's new."

"New? This a serial case? What's this about Amsterdam?"

Adele nodded. "Two other victims."

"Shit."

"Yes. So how can you tell she put up a struggle?"

"One of her fingers is broken," The coroner said blandly. "She was probably trying to pull at whatever the prick throttled her with. Plus, look over there..." Adele followed the coroner's gaze and spotted a high heel shoe discarded by the door.

The other, matching shoe was still on the woman's foot. It didn't take long for Adele to piece it together. She turned, staring at the door, then glancing towards the bed.

"He's strong," she murmured.

"What?" John asked.

"He dragged her from the door to the bed. She tried to fight. But he was too powerful. He's strong—very strong."

"Didn't look like much on film."

"Yeah... maybe that's the point."

She passed a hand through her own dark, blonde hair, frowning towards the corpse. The theory didn't fit. This wasn't a sex-game gone bad. He wasn't randomly targeting strangers in order to get off... Something else was going on here. He'd switched from cautious to reckless. She'd spotted a camera on the way up the stairs, but she didn't doubt he'd likely obscured himself on that film as well.

They were playing a game but didn't know the rules yet.

"Why?" Adele said quietly, staring at the body on the bed. She tilted her head.

Two Belgian women. Very similar in appearance, in height, in career. Was he looking for someone specific? Was the murder a manifestation of his rage at failing his quest?

What quest?

"Love or power... just another word for fear... or money..." she murmured to herself.

"What was that?" John asked.

"Nothing—nothing." She pointed a finger directly at the body on the bed. "This wasn't a crime of opportunity. He knew this woman. Or at least, targeted her. This isn't a sexual *type;* this is a hunt."

"A hunt?"

"Yes, John, a hunt. And I don't think he's found his prey yet."

"Three dead women, Adele. He's doing enough damage already."

She sighed but shook her head, turning towards the door. She paused though and glanced back. "Anything else?"

The coroner looked up again, still clearly irritated by their presence. "What was that?"

"Can you check the woman's hands for prints?" Adele asked.

"Her hands?" the coroner asked.

Adele nodded. "This one put up a struggle. I don't think he was expecting that. The first two didn't. He was able to trick or threaten them. Maybe he has a weapon, I don't know. But if she broke her finger by trying to stop him from throttling her, then he might have made a mistake in the struggle."

Cautious. But reckless. Two sides to this killer.

"Can you check her hands?" Adele repeated.

The woman shrugged one shoulder, then turned to her black satchel, muttering about bossy newcomers beneath her breath.

"What's she saying now?" John whispered.

"Talking about the weather," Adele murmured back.

John nodded as if this made sense. Adele hid a smile and gave him a quick side hug that the coroner didn't notice.

The woman pulled strands of see-through plastic adhesive strips from her kit. She moved from one hand to the next, careful, still breathing like an English bulldog.

Adele waited patiently in the doorway. She heard footsteps behind her as the assistants returned with a stretcher between them on wheels. Adele held up a hand, though, holding them back.

Together, they waited.

And waited...

And then, the coroner looked up.

Adele swallowed nervously. "Anything?"

"Might be nothing," the older woman said slowly.

Adele's heart skipped.

"But I think we have a partial on the poor woman's broken thumb. It looks like the bastard twisted it himself."

"A partial print?" Adele said, her tone rising.

The coroner waved dismissively. "Yes, yes—just a partial though. Might not turn up anything."

"That's fine—more than fine. How long do you think, actually, you know what, can we send those to Interpol, please? They'll expedite."

The coroner grunted and shrugged. "Less work for me. Will still have to scan them here and send them over. Gonna take a while. This isn't like the movies."

Adele nodded in thanks, already turning to leave the room.

John hastened to keep up.

"What happened?" he said. "The ugly one sounded less angry at the end."

"John, keep your voice down. That's rude."

"So was she."

Adele rolled her eyes but couldn't keep her mood sour. Her lips twisted into a thin, grim smile. "We might have a partial print," she said. "On the woman's hand."

"They should send it through Interpol," John said quickly. "Will save time."

"That's what I told her," Adele replied. She gave John a pat on the back. "Look who's paying attention after all."

John snorted, shoving her hand away. "I was doing this long before you showed up, American Princess. Did you notice the camera on the way in? Bet you didn't."

"I did—"

"Definitely didn't."

"I saw the camera J—"

"You're lucky to have me, you know. Let's find the owner—get that footage. Maybe our killer slipped up twice."

CHAPTER FIFTEEN

Night had turned to early morning and now found John and Adele sitting in the parking lot of a fast-food restaurant in a BKA borrowed vehicle.

Adele's eyes drooped and she held back a yawn as she inhaled the odor of greasy French fries and chicken nuggets. John gorged himself on his feast while Adele occasionally ventured to steal a fry or two between sips from the water she'd ordered.

But her appetite just wasn't there.

"Three of them," she said quietly, staring out the window at the gas station across the highway just south of Dortmund.

"Huh?"

"Three victims—all prostitutes. Two Belgian."

John scarfed a fry and nodded to show he was tracking. His phone buzzed, and he glanced down. Through a mouthful of potato mush, he said, "Interpol got the fingerprints."

"Anything yet?"

"Nothing. Gonna take some time."

Adele sighed, crossing her arms and placing a foot on the dash, frowning through the windshield as a semi truck's headlights flashed past. "The second victim, the one called Silver."

"Sasha De Guyne?" John said.

"Yeah, her—she was pretending to be French."

"You thinking maybe she's also Belgian?"

Adele sighed, giving a faint shake of her head. "I'm not sure. Worth a try, right?" She reached towards her pocket, lowering her foot from the dash and pulling out the small, plastic cut-out that the Red Letter owner had provided.

She held it up to her phone's camera and snapped a picture.

"Think Foucault will be up at this hour?"

John snorted. "Wouldn't risk it. Try Paige."

"Oh? She give you a hard time?"

"Old crow yelled in my ear. Yeah," he said eagerly. "Call her. See how she likes it."

Adele rolled her eyes. She decided against John's advice. Her relationship with Agent Paige was always rocky regardless. Instead, she sent the picture to the DGSI tech team. She was sent to voicemail automatically—after hours protocol—and raised her phone, speaking clearly.

"Agent Adele Sharp, working the case in Dortmund. I need you to send this photo to Belgian authorities. Cross-reference with any database. Focusing primarily on sex-workers." She paused, then nodded to herself. Before hanging up, she added, "Make it quick."

Then she lowered her device and shook her head, rolling the window down a bit to catch a breeze and ventilate the car of salt and grease wafting on the air. "Why French, though?" Adele said. "Why pretend to be another nationality?"

John snorted. "Seriously?"

"What?"

"French women are exotic, Adele. People love French hookers."

She blinked. "You think she was pretending to be French to attract clients?"

John winked, leaned in and pecked her on the cheek. "I for one can vouch for French girls."

She reached up, dabbing daintily at a bit of mustard. She wiped it off on John's face, smiling sweetly as she did. But even as she poked fun at her boyfriend, her mind was moving.

If her hunch was right, and all three victims were Belgian... what did that connotate? Was the killer Belgian? He was moving from country to country—none of them Belgium. Some sort of hate crime?

"What if he's looking for someone?" Adele murmured slowly.

But just then her phone began to ring. She frowned, picking it up. Even if the tech team was still in that late at night, it was too early to have heard back from a foreign intelligence team. As she raised the phone, though, she relaxed.

"Hey Dad," she said.

"Hey. I heard you're in my neck of the woods."

Adele's eyebrows flitted up. "Wow—someone still has connections."

The Sergeant grunted on the other line. "I was thinking Saturday."

"What's that?"

"Saturday," he said, sounding irritated. But it wasn't irritation at her. She'd grown to decipher the shadows her father's annoyance came in. Now, he didn't like repeating himself because he was embarrassed. "I— that thing you said. Watching TV over the phone. There's an I Love Lucy rerun. If you want to..." He paused, then quickly said, "Not that I don't have better things to do. Just, you know, you sounded lonely."

Adele tried to keep her amusement in check. For her father, even this amount of vulnerability, though hidden under a heap of deflection, was a huge step forward. "Sure," she said. "Saturday should work. I wish I could stop by," she added, sighing, "But I'm working."

"No problem," he said, more gruffly than when he'd started. And yet he sounded pleased all the same. "Saturday then. I'm looking forward to it."

Adele grinned but kept her tone professional. "Looking forward to it, sir. Talk to you later. Have a good night." She hung up to find John watching her.

"Who was that?" he said.

"Fabio," she replied without missing a beat. "He'll be joining us for that threesome."

John glared, taking a bite out of his hamburger wrapper while distracted and swallowing it without noticing.

At that moment, Renee's phone buzzed again.

Adele looked over. The big man sighed, glancing down, rubbing a smear of mustard off his phone, then winced. "Damn. The print isn't enough. The partial didn't take. They can't track it."

Adele felt her heart plummet. "The coroner sent them what she had, right?"

"Yeah, looks like it. But the take wasn't clean." He turned his phone so Adele could read the email.

Her eyes zipped across the text, and her frustration mounted. Once she'd finished, she slammed her hand against the window, all signs of her earlier good mood vanishing like morning dew. "Shit," she said.

"Shit," John agreed.

"Dammit," she said.

"Dammit," John added, helpfully.

"Christ!"

"Chr—"

"John..."

"Sorry, thought I was helping. You always tell me to let you *feel* your emotions, don't you?"

"No John, that's psychobabble bullshit. I don't keep you around to feel things. I keep you around to punch them." She glared through the windshield, shoving aside the horrifying thought that perhaps she was more like her father than she wanted to admit. Now wasn't the time for such horrible realizations.

But without a print, they were no closer to figuring out the killer's identity.

"Think we should get some sleep?" John asked.

"I mean... it's nearly two. Not like we have anything else. Is the club operating tomorrow?"

"Yeah—runs all week."

Adele sighed. She massaged her temples. "Hopefully we can hear back from the Belgians come morning. If not..." she trailed off, shaking her head. "I don't know what to do, John."

"He'll probably kill again," John said with a shrug. "Maybe he'll screw up. He was messier this last time."

Adele scowled, rolling the window down all the way now and listening to the sound of traffic. "I don't want him to *screw up*. That means he kills again. No more, John. He gets three, but that's it."

John seemed to realize she wasn't in the joking mood and instead put the car in gear, pulling them out of the fast-food parking lot and turning onto the highway.

Adele could feel her mood souring once more. Her stomach twisted as she stared through the glass. The call from the Belgian authorities would have to bring answers. They needed a nudge, a clue—*something*.

CHAPTER SIXTEEN

Adele's night had passed without dreams. As she groaned, pushing off the stiff, cheap hotel bed, she paused to inhale slowly and appreciate a full night of rest without interruption by her usual slew of nightmares.

Something about her conversation with John, back at his place, had lifted a burden of guilt from her shoulders—not completely, but it felt a bit easier to carry the load. She stifled a yawn with an open hand and listed to the faint hum of traffic just outside her window. She paused, though, still drowsy and trying to place a different sound—distinct from the cacophony through her window.

Her gaze shifted towards the bed, and her heart skipped. The phone was lighting up on the dresser. Adele nearly tripped over the edge of the bed in her haste to reach the device. She panted as she slapped the cold glass to her cheek. "Yes?"

"Agent Sharp?"

"Foucault, sir?"

"We got your request last night," the executive said.

"I—yes, sir. I meant to contact the tech team. I didn't mean to bother you—"

"International information requests have to be approved by my office." He didn't sound irritated, just tired. "We have a hit."

Adele went quiet suddenly, prickles on her cheeks. "Who?" she said but had to speak louder as the first word barely came as a whisper. She cleared her throat. "Who, sir?"

"That ID you sent," Foucault replied. "There's a match. Our second victim was apparently arrested for prostitution in Belgium but fled the country before her court date."

"And this most recent victim, sir? From the FKK club?"

"Also vanished from Belgium and ended up in Germany."

Adele pumped her fist but kept her tone professional. "Thank you, sir. Anything else?"

"Not on my end. Does this help the case?"

"I—I think so. Thank you, sir."

She waited for Foucault to hang up, then gripped her device, cycling through her contacts. At the same time, juggling the phone, she hastily got dressed and then rushed to the hotel room door while already calling Agent Renee.

A sleepy voice answered. "You get the call?" he said.

"I—wait, did they call you?"

"Email," he said.

"Where are you?"

"Pulling the car around," John replied with a grunt.

"Good—good," Adele said quickly. She was breathing heavily as she circled a cheap, faux-wood banister, moving towards the stairs. "We need to head back to that club."

"Yeah? What are you thinking?"

"All three girls were Belgian," Adele said. "Two of our victims fled the country because of prostitution."

John grunted. "Think we'll find another at the club?"

"I think we might have a chance of finding *how* these women are crossing the border and setting up shop in new countries. Just hang tight, I'll be right there."

Adele took the stairs two at a time. Her phone slipped back into her pocket, the skin on her fingers occasionally squeaking against the lacquered banister as she hastened to the parking lot.

***

The club looked far less accommodating beneath the wink of sunlight. The parking lot behind the brothel was nearly empty. No sound of music pulsed from the building. A few caterers and stockers moved in and out of a steel, rear door as Adele and John moved around the front of the building.

"They said the owner would meet us on the first floor," John advised as they moved beneath a black awning and across tiled ground with glinting pieces of metal sparkling thanks to overhead lighting. It would have been quite pretty if Adele hadn't known what this place was for.

Not just a brothel, but a brothel that used women in dire straits. Desperate women searching for a paycheck. Granted, not all the women were innocent in this either. It was easy to try and blame one person's sexual appetite while ignoring another's financial one. John didn't mind places like this, but for Adele, having dealt with so many victims of violence over the years, she knew clubs that catered in skin were often prime hunting grounds for the sort of killer they were currently pursuing.

She set her expression, hiding her unease as she followed John into the first level.

Waiting there was a man in a purple hat with a big, oiled goatee and a fur coat wrapped over his neck. The man was talking to one of the bartenders, shaking his head and finger in an exaggerated fashion. "No, no," the man with the hat said, "not back there. We're trying to make a profit, remember? Keep the good stuff visible."

The bartender nodded quickly, and bottles clinked as he moved items on the shelf.

Adele cleared her throat. But the ostentatious goateed fellow didn't glance over. "Hello!" John said, always the more direct of the two.

The man turned, frowning, but then his plucked eyebrows flitted up. "Oh, yes. DGSI, right? Agent Adele Sharp by way of Paris, Hamburg, and San Francisco. And..." he pressed a finger to his chin, looking John up and down as if examining a runway model. "Agent John Renee, ex-special forces. How might I help you two?"

Adele blinked, shooting a look at John. He gave a little shake of his head.

"Oh, don't look at him, darling. I do my own research. I'm Klaud. You may call me Klaud."

"Alright, Mr. Klaud," Adele said, carefully.

"No, no, dear. Just Klaud. How can I help you so very, very..." he paused and rolled his eye, "*very* early in the morning?"

Adele glanced at her watch. It was nearly ten AM. She decided not to counter him on this point. "We wanted to speak with some of your girls," Adele replied, leaning against a cold, glass table, and studying the club owner.

He flashed a smile, his teeth as bright as an advertisement. "Wonderful. Which girl?"

"All of them," John replied.

The man's smiled faded.

Adele quickly amended, "The foreign girls. Anyone from out of country. How many are currently here?"

"Well..." he sighed, "A few are on staff currently. Most will come later tonight. Some are off until next weekend. They work on a contracting basis, not as salaried employees. I'm sure you understand." He gave a little giggle. "Restaurant industry."

"Right. Restaurant," Adele said.

"What we do here is perfectly legal," he shot back, watching her closer now.

Adele didn't comment on this point. She shrugged. "Do you have any foreign girls here now?"

"A few... a few. Yes. I don't exactly check, you know. If they're able to work, they're able to work. Accent and background are irrelevant." He winked at John. "I'm sure you know what I mean."

Adele sighed, forging ahead and trying to keep them all on track. "Where might we be able to speak with them?"

"Where? Hmm. Oh... Well, how long do you think—"

"As long as it takes. You can open for business when we're done," Adele said without even blinking.

The man's smile slipped completely now. He muttered something beneath his breath, but then waved at an area across the dance floor. "VIP rooms," he said, sounding bored now. "I'll have Karle fetch the girls. It might take a few minutes. We don't normally look at *race...* "

"This isn't about race," Adele shot back. "It's about country of origin in order to protect these women. Please hurry."

Tight-lipped, stiff-armed, she turned and marched away, moving across the slick dance floor, beneath more than one rotating silver orb dangling from the ceiling. John padded hurriedly after her without making comment.

They reached a long, red rope cordoning off the VIP rooms. Adele pushed through first, stepping around the golden stanchion. John just stepped over the thing as if it wasn't even there. They entered a small alcove of a room with purple couches and glitter stains along the marble floor. A privacy curtain was half-pulled over the space and a couple of framed, glass photos on the wall displayed images of B-rate German celebrities Adele had never heard of who probably visited the club.

John collapsed on one of the couches, his arms spread across the top. He flung his legs up on a metal table and leaned back with a faint sigh.

Adele glanced at the glitter, at the couch, and then remained standing, moving off to the side so she could face the opening in the curtain.

"You look relaxed," she muttered.

John shrugged. "Been a while since I've been in a place like this—I mean. This is a very weird place. Wow. So strange."

Adele snorted. "You think you're funny. You *think.*"

John snorted. "I can't hear you over the sound of my good joke."

She tried to hide a grin and was aided by the approaching sound of tapping high heels. She wiped her face of any expression, cleared her throat, and faced the opening in the curtain. John also sat up straight, adjusting his wrinkled suit shirt.

The first woman who entered had a shaved head and too much eyeshadow. Her lips were pursed, her cheeks sharp like a supermodel's, and she wore what amounted to a business suit with lace visible just past the collar.

Behind her, three other women approached, navigating up the single step from the dance floor to the VIP rooms, looking nervously around as they drew near.

"Thank you for coming," Adele said quickly, nodding at each in turn. Behind her back, she waved towards John to scoot over. The big man did, making room on the purple couch. Cautiously, the four women slowly sat, crossing their legs modestly and remaining alert.

"There is no polite way to start," Adele said, "But I'm assuming none of you are native to Germany."

The women all shot each other startled looks.

"I'm not here about that," Adele said. "I just need to ask some questions."

The woman in the business suit frowned, her lips pursed. The others, younger, seemed to be taking their cues from her and also went quiet.

Adele frowned. "I don't want to cause trouble. I just need some information."

The silence continued.

"If we have to, we can go to background checks. If criminal records are found it could be grounds for extradition."

The woman in the suit narrowed her eyes. One of the younger women with blonde curls leaned in whispering something.

"Deportation," the older woman said. "That's what extradition means. They'll kick us out of Germany." She had a very strong accent as she spoke. Romanian? Adele wasn't sure.

She zeroed in on this woman. "I'm not trying to cause trouble," Adele insisted. "I just need some help..." She inhaled slowly, then added, "I'm trying to find the man who killed your friend. He's killed others. Help me. Please," she added.

The older woman just glared, but the one with the blonde curls suddenly let out a little gasp. She shook her head, her hair bouncing. She raised a hand as if she were in school.

"Umm, yes..." Adele nodded at her.

"I knew Monique!"

"I'm sorry for your loss," Adele said, keeping her tone even. "I'm told she came here to beat an arrest. She never showed up for court. How..." She trailed off, piecing her words together, as delicate as they would be. "How might one go about doing that? Crossing the border. Setting up in a place like this. Room. Board. All of it."

The older woman shot a narrow-eyed look back at Blonde Curls. But the threat of extradition seemed to have done it.

"I can't go back," the young woman said, shaking her head. "Please. Do not make me."

"That's not my intention. You have my word."

"I—I don't know much. But I... umm... arrived..." she paused, trailing off.

Adele nodded to show she understood without forcing the woman to spell it out. "You arrived..." she pressed.

"Yes. Umm. Yes, around the same time as Monique. I—we... we had some help," she mumbled.

Another one of the women hissed sharply, got to her feet and marched out of the VIP room without a second look back.

Adele didn't watch her leave; she focused on the blonde lady. "Help? What sort of help?"

"I—just..."

"Petra, quiet!" the older woman hissed. "You'll get us all in trouble."

But Petra shifted along the couch, away from the ringleader, and blurted out suddenly as if afraid she might be stopped, "A man. A Turkish man. He arranged everything—papers, rooms—everything!"

"This man helped both of you?"

"Yes! Yes! He's not bad. Not really. Please—please don't tell him I told you." She looked suddenly panicked, a manicured hand with red nails darting to her chest as if making sure her heart hadn't escaped.

"This man, does he have a name?"

"I... I don't know."

"I need his name."

"No—I, no name," she said, wincing as she did and shaking her head quickly.

"Petra, you need to help me, *please,*" Adele said, thinking of the three other women who weren't so lucky to still be drawing breath.

But Petra looked panicked now, her long paste-on eyelashes fluttering. She hyperventilated and kept shooting glances off past the curtain.

Adele bit her lip, considering her options. She didn't like the heavy-handed approach. She didn't want to scare any of the women. But on the other hand, lives were at stake. Still... it didn't feel good following up with, "You've just admitted you used a trafficker to come to

Germany. If I check your papers, if I get BKA to check, what will come up?" Adele wanted to bite her tongue, but she kept her composure even as her stomach twisted.

The woman's look of shock, of fear. was enough to make Adele queasy. But Petra stammered, "I—you said—no! I don't know name! I don't!"

"You said the same man brought you and Monique here. You might not know a name, but you can get me in contact with him, can't you?"

Suddenly, the tall woman in the business suit with hints of lace pushed to her feet. She frowned at Adele, but reached into her pocket, pulling out a small, folded business card stack. She undid a red rubber-band, sorted through the cards for a second, then emerged with an off-white rectangle of paper.

"Here," she said insistently, shoving it towards Adele. "Leave us alone. We told you nothing," she said, raising an eyebrow significantly.

Adele glanced at the paper. A name. Baris, on top. And a phone number.

"This is what I need?" Adele said, raising the paper between two fingers. "I can come back if it isn't."

"That is what you need," the woman insisted. She helped Petra to her feet and along with the other women quickly pushed back out of the VIP room with practiced haste, leaving Adele holding a small strip of paper and feeling sick to her stomach.

"Damn it," she muttered once the women had hurried away. She faintly detected the sound of high heels retreating.

"All good?" John asked, who hadn't understood a word of the accented German.

"No," she murmured. "Not really." She studied the name and number on the otherwise blank paper. "Then again, this might be our point of contact."

She handed the card to John as he also arose from his seat. "What is it?" he murmured.

"Business card for someone named Baris. A Turkish trafficker."

"Shit. Same guy who got our last victim into the country?"

"Yeah. Looks like. And maybe our second victim, the fake Frenchwoman used a similar service. Maybe even the same guy."

"Think so?"

Adele jammed her hands into her pockets, feeling dirty all of a sudden. "I can think of one way to find out," she said.

"Traffickers can be dangerous, Adele," John advised. He wiggled the business card. "Might want to make a call or two before contacting

Mister... Baris," he finished, reading the name off the card.

"Yeah. Yeah, I was thinking the same thing. Haven't set up a sting on traffickers before." Adele let out an amused huff of air. "Sounds like your type of thing."

John snorted. "It *is* my type of thing. Just sit back and watch, American Princess. We'll have these guys in a cell by nightfall."

CHAPTER SEVENTEEN

The survivor sat outside the pink café at the foot of the DGSI headquarters. He wasn't smiling, but to passing traffic it might have seemed like it. Three facial surgeries, part of the hundreds of hours spent beneath the knife, piecing his corpse back together.

His lips on the left side curved in a perpetual grin, revealing the top two teeth in his mouth. His eyes though, held only hatred.

He peered through the tinted window of his vehicle. Thirty-eight seconds.

That's how long he had before he needed to move. Security cameras watched the road. Officers inside would investigate a vehicle stalled for longer than a minute. They'd take note of one stalled just under that.

But thirty-eight seconds?

That was how long the café's supply truck parked on the curb, perfectly blocking his sedan from the second floor security camera. He'd studied the place at a distance for nearly a week.

Now, though, it was time to act.

He watched as a car rolled into the large parking structure, curling up the asphalt ramp. The concrete bollards slowly rose back into place, creating the first line of defense. He shifted his shoulders, wincing as the scars up his side, along his back twisted.

He hissed in agony but didn't react to it. What could he do? He lived with pain now. He refused medication—refused pills. The pain kept him sharp for what needed to be done.

Would this be the spot? Captain John Renee would feel safe on home turf—would lower his guard surrounded by so many armed protectors.

But Renee was a slippery customer—the survivor knew that much.

The truck by the café sputtered, creaked, then began to move, the tires whirring.

That was his cue.

He put his sedan into gear and slipped into the stream of traffic, using the rear bumper to block his vehicle, picking up speed to then use the truck itself to hide him from view.

Not once would he have appeared on camera.

A ghost.

Just how he'd been trained to be.

How John had trained him.

Now, though, picking up speed, faster, faster, he left rubber on the road, moving up the highway, heading back towards the city.

One potential location for the grab. It would be exhilarating—and he was nothing if not an adrenaline junkie.

But the plan had to *succeed.* That was more important than the thrill.

Which meant what?

He let out a little puff of air, squeezing the steering wheel with the three remaining fingers on his right hand. Another option was available.

John Renee's file suggested he'd made something of a name for himself working as a fed. A strong closure rate in no small part due to his partner, Agent Adele Sharp.

He glanced at the seat next to him, studying the pretty blonde woman. He snorted, shaking his head. Renee always did have the best luck when it came to partners.

There was no way in hell Renee and that woman weren't bumping uglies. That wasn't John's style.

Would she be a vector to cause maximum suffering?

He reached out with his three-fingered hand, brushing the glossy headshot aside to reveal another, far more candid image.

A photo he'd taken outside Claudia's school.

John Renee's daughter.

Shit. He hadn't *had* a daughter when things had gone down in the sandy hellhole where he'd been left behind. But a daughter; John hadn't been the marrying sort, or the siring kind.

This was what made it so difficult to hurt Renee.

Who to go after first?

Eenie-meenie...minie...

He glanced from one photo to the other. The child or the agent? She really was quite pretty. He could think of a few things he might do, on video, sending them to Agent Renee. That might get the big man's attention.

Then again, a missing child? A gut punch. Even to an iron-hearted soldier like Renee.

The big man was a bastard.

But the survivor, over the last ten years, being stitched back together with spit and prayers and surgeon's needles, had learned to be a bastard himself.

It hadn't started with him, but he was sure as hell going to end it.

He floored the pedal, zipping in and out of traffic so fast, the drivers he startled didn't even have time to lean on their horns. He felt a familiar prickle of adrenaline. One of the only things that ever dulled his pain.

Faster. Faster.

Nearly 212 km/h. He gritted his teeth, feeling a rush. Captain Renee had started all of this shit. But he'd end it, in his own damn time.

He had time, now. Enough to make it hurt. To *really* hurt.

Renee thought he knew pain, but the survivor was intent on introducing him to a whole new level.

Tires squealed as he spun onto the shoulder, just because he could. He leaned on his horn as he zipped around a squad car, laughing as he did.

His plates wouldn't match.

The car flashed its lights but was already far in the rearview mirror.

The survivor ripped up the offramp, spinning onto the bridge. The cop was already history. It would be surprising if law enforcement even figured out where he'd gone. Not that it mattered. The car was stolen. He'd ditch it in the next couple minutes down by the river at his planned extraction zone. Two outlets—sewers, or old drainage ditch. If not that, then the woods.

He always came with a plan.

He glanced back at the photos on the seat next to him, exhaling faintly, narrowing his eyes and leaning painfully back in the seat as he rushed around the curve in the ramp and sped through a stop sign.

He couldn't even hear the sound of sirens behind him. Just too damn slow.

CHAPTER EIGHTEEN

Adele tapped her foot nervously as she watched the police moving outside the Dortmund-based precinct. Four cars, eight officers and an unmarked sedan for John. BKA would be running a drone to keep an eye on things.

When they'd called for backup, Adele hadn't expected *this* much. Clearly, trafficking was somewhere on a bureaucrat's *to-do* list.

It wasn't the cops, the radio chatter, or the repeated instructions to the new arrivals from Agent Renee that bothered her. It was the man in an old, blue uniform, with a drooping, walrus mustache and a bit of a bow-legged walk marching towards her.

She felt uneasy-happy, like always when her dad showed up.

John's voice carried on the afternoon air as he addressed the cops in English, "Agent Sharp will be going in first. If anyone catches a whiff of you, the whole thing will bust. We don't want scattered traffickers."

Adele listened vaguely to the plan she and John had already gone over three times on their drive to the precinct. Renee hated the idea of using Adele as bait, but they'd done it before, and it had turned out good enough.

Now, though, John's voice faded into the background as her gaze landed once more on her father.

The Sergeant marched stiffly towards her, his thumbs looped inside his black belt buckle. His weapon on his hip.

"Hey Dad," Adele said, trying to sound cheerful. "Catching me in a bit of a, er, moment."

"I heard," he said gruffly. "I want to help." Then, still somewhat stiff, he stepped in hurriedly and hugged her, releasing just as quickly. It felt like planks of wood patting her along the shoulders, and yet it was the tenderest greeting she'd had from her father in a long while.

"Umm, thanks," she said. Then realizing it might make things awkward to show gratitude for something as simple as a hug, she hastily addressed his comment. "I—I don't know if we need the backup, Dad."

"Nonsense, I'm coming."

His tone didn't leave much room for argument.

"Well, Renee's going to be in the SUV," she said. "I'm sure he won't mind having a German-speaker with him. Most of the cops speak English, though. Just to keep comms clear."

Her father bobbed his head. "Rainy will be safe with me."

Adele smirked at the mispronunciation of John's last name. She hid it though, and fished her phone from her pocket, double-checking the pre-programmed number.

"Am I hearing the big guy right?" the Sergeant asked. "You're posing as a hooker?"

Adele raised an eyebrow. "I'll be safe."

"Psh. Not worried about that. Kinda... scandalous, isn't it?"

She stared. "Dad... I'm not *actually* a prostitute."

"No, no I know that. Of course." He waved a hand dismissively, but still seemed a bit more at ease at this comment.

Adele tried not to roll her eyes, but sometimes it was an absolute mystery trying to figure out how that man's brain worked. No matter; he'd stiff-hugged her and come to help. If that wasn't the Sharp household version of a big, sloppy *I love you,* then nothing was.

She glanced over at John who was wrapping up the final comments. One of the officers was leaning towards another and repeating some of the harder-to-understand words in German.

Another cop shot a look towards Adele, hesitantly.

She turned her back on the gathering, facing away from the cars and the uniformed officers. She lifted her phone, moved further away from the parking lot until she could no longer hear chatter behind her. She glanced up and down the street to make sure no cop cars were incoming that might accidentally flare their siren, and then she raised her phone, staring at the number she'd transposed from the business card.

She swallowed, wetting her dry lips with her tongue. "Here goes nothing," she murmured.

She pressed dial. And waited.

The phone rang twice. Three times. Four. She glanced back to see her father frowning towards her. She flashed a thumbs up and an uneasy smile. He crossed his arms over his barrel chest.

She looked back towards the asphalt, counting quietly in her head if only to keep herself calm. Another ring. Another.

Then.

Silence. Nothing. Adele frowned, beginning to lower the phone to make sure she hadn't accidentally disconnected, but then, she heard a faint rasp.

The phone darted back to her ear. "H—hello?" she said in French.

A louder, rasping sound. Heavy breathing on the other line.

"Hello, please," Adele said, injecting a bit more fear in her tone. This took some doing. She wasn't *scared* of whoever was on the other line. She was scared about losing the lead, though. Scared about letting the killer find a fourth victim. "I—I was told to call this number," she said, continuing in French. Then, she switched to English, but put on a heavy, broken accent. "Please. Sir, please. Please do hear me you?"

Another long exhale. Then, a reply, in neat, tidy English. An educated voice. "Yes, my dear—who gave you this number?"

Adele swallowed. She couldn't out the women at the FKK club. So she took a gamble. "Monique," she said. The third victim. There wouldn't be reprisals on a dead woman.

The phone clicked off.

Adele waited, heart pounding. She checked the screen. Disconnected. He'd hung up.

"Shit!" she said. "Shit. Shit. Dammit!"

She hesitated, finger hovering over the green dial button, wondering if she ought to call again. But before she could, her phone began to vibrate. An incoming call. From a different number. The ID was blocked. A secure line?

She raised her phone, answering. "Hello? Hello—please!" This time, she didn't need to fake the desperation.

"Listen closely," the voice said. "Who are you and what do you need?"

"Please—I need to get back to France," Adele said hurriedly. "I—I have no money. I don't... I work..." She feigned shame, swallowing as she did.

"A working lady? I understand. Where are you now?"

"Dortmund," she said quickly. "Just outside of Dortmund."

"Perfect. It's going to be expensive up front..." he trailed off, allowing it to sink in. Adele wondered how many times he'd practiced the timing. She knew traffickers like this didn't have to take fees up front. Often, they had other ways of making their money.

"Or," he said, once he'd allowed the supposed dread to linger, "We can reach a bit of an agreement."

"Yes, please!" Adele said. "Anything. I—what do I do?"

"Half. All your earnings. Five years. Understand? If you skimp, I send a guy to have a chat. It won't be a nice chat. If you skimp twice, your legs. Three times, the river. Understand me?"

Adele swallowed. Now, the untraceable number made sense. "Yes. I—I understand. Please. I need to get to France tonight."

"You need papers?"

"Yes!"

"That's another five percent. Or two thousand up-front."

"No—I can't pay."

"Fifty-five percent, then. We've got people in France, too. Now listen carefully, I'll send some guys for you. I'm texting an address. You have to show up *blindfolded.* Understand? If you're not, or if you bring anyone else, we'll see it and leave. I'll never answer another call from you. I've already recorded your voice. Trust me. I'll remember."

Adele felt a faint shiver prickle up her spine at these words. Even though she knew she held all the cards, the man's tone suggested otherwise, and he knew it.

She felt a flicker of vindictive enjoyment at the chance of sticking it to someone like this.

"Alright—blindfold. I can do that. Where?"

"Sending the address now. Remember. Come alone. We'll figure out details there. You might have to make a good faith payment up front."

"What sort of payment?" Adele said, eyes narrowing.

"Don't worry—nothing too tough for a working girl. Meet us at that address." Her phone buzzed and then the man on the other end hung up.

Adele glanced down at the coordinates Baris had sent. She clicked the hyperlink and her phone's map app opened up to a long stretch of nowhere on a German back road, twenty miles south.

She felt a faint shiver down her spine. How many women had agreed to this sort of deal? People would do desperate things in desperate situations.

How many women hadn't made it out alive?

She shivered at the thought, eyes narrowing. This was a lead for her case, but it was also an opportunity to put a bad guy behind bars.

She lowered her phone, turning back to face the parking lot full of police. John, her father and eight armed cops all watched her. She felt a flicker of gratitude at all the back-up. John was waving a bulletproof vest like a flag, gesturing at Adele to approach and grab it.

She flashed a quick thumbs up and nodded. Sliding her phone back into her pocket, she hurried over towards where John was waiting.

"We good to go?"

"Yeah. Good. Just... I'm going to need a blindfold too."

John frowned at this, biting his tongue, but then saying, quickly, "I still don't think you should—"

"You want to?" she said, raising an eyebrow. "One look at you and they're gone, John. It has to be me."

"Let me guess," Renee muttered beneath his breath. "You have to come alone."

Adele winced, shrugged once but gave a quick nod.

John let out a long sigh, pushing the vest into Adele's hands and growling, "I'll find a blindfold.... Shit," he added as an afterthought before turning and stalking away.

Adele was already moving towards her tinted, beaten-up sedan she'd be using. An old, rusted hunk of junk. The second, cleaner sedan would follow as close as it could, with her father and Renee. The cops would also keep their distance.

She slipped into the front seat, breathing heavily, shut the door for privacy, and then, in the back, hidden by the windows, she began to unbutton her shirt to place on the vest. A bullet to the chest—she'd survive. To the head, though?

There were a lot of ways this might go bad. BKA would keep surveillance in the sky, but the desolate road would make approaching it difficult.

She exhaled slowly, pulling her shirt back on over the vest.

Still, this had to be done. Baris had known one of the victims. If anyone could find information on their fake Frenchwoman, it would be him. If this was the only way to connect the dots, then Adele didn't see a choice.

***

Adele peered through the now dusty windshield, eyes on the open road. A metal barrier had been removed at the intersection where she'd taken a turn off the main highway onto what at first had resembled a service road... but it just kept going.

Her phone beeped as she neared the dot on the map. Nothing ahead of her. Nothing behind. Some vegetation, dirt, an old billboard that had been mostly torn down save the support structure.

The tires ground to a halt, kicking dirt and asphalt in equal measures. A cloud of dust arose behind her, obscuring her vision.

Adele glanced up, through the sunroof towards the mid-afternoon sky.

A flash of something... The drone?

She had to remember she was being watched. Back-up was there for her. Fear would only get in the way.

She adjusted her shirt, double-checking the top button. The vest was thinner than usual. It wouldn't stand up to any large caliber rifle. But she wasn't expecting military hardware for a trafficking run.

Still, one could never be too prepared.

She unbuttoned her holster, sliding it into the glove compartment. She made sure her ID and badge were hidden from view as well. They might check the car, but by then it would be too late.

She just needed them to show.

Adele brushed her hair behind one ear, dabbing faintly at the receiver.

"Can you hear me?" John's voice echoed in her head.

"Got you," she said, trying not to move her lips. "I don't see them."

John paused. Another voice said, "Try leaving the car." John sighed at this request, clearly unhappy, but Adele knew what she had to do.

She slipped from the front seat, closing the door behind her as she stepped into the middle of the dusty road. She waved a hand in front of her face, clearing the lingering residue, her nose itching.

She held her breath as the dust and dirt settled, peering up and down the road.

"Blindfold," John reminded her.

Adele let out a shaky sigh, but reached into her pocket, pulling out the ripped black fabric from one of John's old t-shirts. It still smelled like his aftershave. She lifted it, examining it for a moment and using this as an excuse to quickly survey the surrounding scene. The only object of interest was the dilapidated billboard.

There, from the metal platform, she thought she spotted a glimmer.

"Glass," Adele murmured quietly. She pressed the blindfold to her eyes. "Might be a camera watching me."

"Be careful," John said. "The moment we spot them, we're coming."

Adele nodded, hoping the drone footage would pick it up. She tied the blindfold off, then stood awkwardly by her rusted SUV, waiting.

No sounds of traffic. No approaching voices.

She was blind for the moment, the cotton pressed against her eyelids. She could still see her feet along the slant of her nose. She took a shuffling step back, off the road, just in case a car came by.

"Adele," John's voice again. "Adele, I think you're right. They have eyes on you. We're watching a couple of cars further down the road. They were waiting at a rest stop."

"Two cars?" Adele said, heart-pounding.

"Yeah," John's voice crackled. "Picking up speed. It's them, Adele. We're coming."

"No!" she said firmly. "We don't know it's them. Don't move until I have confirmation."

"Christ, Adele—don't be stupid. Go in!" John's voice echoed. "Now—go!"

"No!" Adele commanded, sharply but quietly. "You'll ruin this, John. I need to confirm it's them."

"Dammit, Adele. It's two cars off a rest stop. Expensive Mercedes. It's them. They started moving the moment you put the blindfold on. It's them!"

Adele kept her teeth set. "Not until I can ID them," she snapped. "John, trust me."

Her partner growled in frustration, and it sounded like he'd smacked the dashboard. Her father wasn't chiming in now, ever the professional. He would know to keep radio silence while command hashed out the orders.

Still, it was unnerving to know her father was watching all of this.

She tapped her fingers against her chest, just making sure the vest was still there.

Now, she thought she heard the grinding of tires against dirt. The sound of an approaching vehicle, from the opposite direction she'd come from. What was even out there? They'd checked the maps, but the rest stop was all they'd seen for miles.

"Come on," she murmured softly. "Come on..."

She stood there, eyes blind, unarmed, the perfect bait for men like this. She'd even let her hair down, her blonde locks catching the breeze.

She heard the squeak of tires. Silence. Then slamming doors. Booted feet.

"Who did you call?" A voice demanded.

Not a voice she recognized.

"Adele?" John's voice in her ear.

"Not yet," she murmured, ever so quietly. "He's not here," she whispered. "I don't think he came."

"Adele—enough. I'm coming."

She turned, pretending to cough from the dust, but said in a fierce hiss. "Stay back, Agent Renee. Stay back until I confirm the voice."

"Who did you call?" the same demand as the booted feet approached. She glimpsed thick, leather boots appearing just within her line of sight down the slant of her nose. Four feet. Two men. Were others waiting in the car?

She heard voices now, from further back. More than two assailants.

"Baris," Adele said quickly. "Baris was who I called."

"You have payment?" one of the men demanded. She felt a rough hand grab at her shoulder, tugging hard.

"N-not yet," she stammered.

This man wasn't Baris. He wasn't the man in charge. She needed to speak with the leader of the outfit to find out what he knew about Amsterdam. About the dead Belgian. If she called in the cavalry now, she'd lose her opportunity.

"There are other ways to pay," the man whispered in her ear. A native German by the sound of things. A hired thug. His fingers dug into her shoulder, tugging her forward. Her first thought was to the tightening of her sleeve and shirt from the friction. If they spotted the outline of the bulletproof vest, things would rapidly escalate.

"I've got the pay," Adele said quickly, thinking on her feet. "But I can only give it to Baris. I can transfer it to him. It's in my account."

The man with his fingers digging in her shoulder snorted. "Pay now. Up front."

"I—no. I didn't bring cash. The banks would have looked at me funny." She suddenly realized she was speaking too quickly, too fluently. She needed to match the voice she'd used on the phone. She was using an accent, but in her excitement, was losing it. She forced herself to inhale shakily, then said, "Baris would want the money himself. I can only transfer it to him."

The man released his grip from her shoulder, grumbling. His boots crunched dirt as he stepped back and began muttering with the other man. She picked up the German easily enough but pretended like she didn't.

"Let's just have some fun," one of the men was saying. "She's a whore. It's what she does."

"Baris doesn't do that," the other man replied. "If she has payment, that's it. Last guy who cost him his reputation got his tongue pulled out his neck."

The first man snorted. "Moron thinks he's running a business. Reputation? Please. These women are desperate."

Adele cleared her throat. "Baris said I could pay later," she lied. "I can wire it to him when I see him."

The men paused, then continued their muttered conference. As they spoke, Adele turned, breathing shakily. "John?" she whispered, waving a hand in front of her moving lips as if she were clearing dust. "I'm going to get them to make a call. Trace it. Then come in."

A crackle. "Got it."

"Check with him," she said, louder. "We already reached an agreement. Just call him."

She waited quietly. The two men grumbled some more, but then one said. "Wait." Louder, he added, "Don't touch her until I get back."

Then he stomped away, grumbling as he left. A second later, which felt like an eternity, the man started to speak. A quieter, more respectful tone. The sort of voice one might use with a boss...

She waited, wetting her lips. "Wait until he hangs up," she whispered.

"What was that?" the second man asked.

Adele winced. Blindfolded, she'd lost track of the backup goon. "Umm, nothing," she said.

"No—you said something." The man snapped. His shadow shifted across her blindfold. He leaned in and she felt a hand against her cheek. The fingers moved towards her ear. "What is this... Holy... what is..."

The voice further up the road went silent. Booted feet returning. He'd hung up. He'd made the call, then hung up.

"John!" Adele shouted. She reached up, ripped off her blindfold and shoved the man closest to her, *hard*.

As she stared at the two men, her eyes darted towards the vehicles behind them. Two more figures were quickly getting out, weapons in hand.

"Shit," she muttered, standing on the dusty road, unarmed, facing four gun-toting traffickers.

CHAPTER NINETEEN

John didn't need a second invitation. His eyes were glued to the video feed on his tablet from the BKA drone. The moment Adele shoved the man, though, he was screaming into the radio. "Go! Go! Go! Jam communications. Now! Jam them!"

John might not have been as thrilled about this plan as Adele, but he was no rookie. He understood the play well enough. The head honcho wasn't around. Adele had been stalling. They'd placed a call which the German cops were tracking. Now, if they placed any *other* calls to warn their boss, it might spook him.

John raced from the shoulder of the road, slamming through a closed metal barrier along what resembled a service road, leading four cop cars behind him. Ahead, he glimpsed the faint sheen of the low-flying drone.

A cloud of dust had been churned up along the road, but further down, he spotted figures moving in the dark cloud.

"Dammit!" he yelled.

The Sergeant was sitting next to him. The old, beer-bellied brute was glaring through the window, his hand on his weapon, his eyes narrowed and glinting like steel. The man knew how to keep his trap shut, but John recognized that look. A look he'd seen on more than his share of service men—that was the look they got when a battle turned personal.

Not that John minded.

He floored the pedal, the second SUV roaring up the path.

Through the cloud of dust, amidst the shouting figures, it took him a second to place Adele. She was standing, a man kneeling at her feet, clutching his crotch and vomiting in the dirt. Somehow, she'd already cuffed him.

Three other men were sprinting back towards their cars, shouting at each other and gesturing towards the approaching cops.

John didn't put on the brakes but instead decided to stop the car in a less conventional way. He barreled straight into one of the sleek, silver Mercedes, denting the side, trapping the driver's door. At the same time, jolting, head rattling, John shoved open the front door and sprinted towards the second Mercedes.

He hopped the hood, sliding across it.

Two shots. Bullets through the window. John kept low, his head beneath the line of glass. More shouting from in the car. Another shot. The window above him shattered.

Crystal fragments scattered across his upraised arm, and along his back, tapping to the ground in a glimmering shower.

John made a rumbling growl, reached up with one arm, his head still ducked beneath the window, and snatched at whatever he first touched inside the driver's seat, through the now blasted window.

He caught a shirt and ripped *hard.*

With a shout, a man was pulled bodily from inside the car. John ripped the fellow through the shattered glass window, his muscles straining. With a yell John slammed the man to the ground.

The beady-eyed trafficker gasped, his gun clattering beneath the car. John punched him, knocking him out with a swift knuckle shot to the temple. Then he surged to his feet, staring wild-eyed through the door.

The final trafficker had a gun raised, aiming through the window. His hand was trembling. This last guy looked young.

John had time to duck, but instead he just went still, glaring through the window. He slowly raised a hand, but instead of putting his palm up he just pointed at the trafficker's trembling gun.

"Put it down," he said, injecting as much venom as he could into the words. "Now!"

The giant Frenchman, covered in dust, who'd just ripped a man through a window, glared, his scar rippling as he inhaled a shaky breath. Something feral, invigorating, swelled through his body. Part of him wondered if he could jump through the window and take the gun-toting fool before he got off a shot.

"I said," John repeated, slow and ominous. "Put it down."

Sirens were flashing all around them now. Cops were hastily swarming the scene. But the man in the Mercedes only had eyes for Renee. He stared, he squeaked, then dropped the weapon.

It bounced off his leg and fell beneath the seat.

"I—I--I didn't... Please don't hurt me," the man mewled.

John pointed at his head. "Get out of the car," he snapped.

The man did.

"On the ground! Hands behind your back. Don't you dare move!"

John gestured at one of the nearest cops, miming cuffs over his wrists and pointing to the prone trafficker and his unconscious compatriot.

Two Germans nodded and hastened over. John, meanwhile, hurtled the hood of the car again and sprinted back in the direction of Adele, his heart hammering.

The man she'd kneed in the crotch was being cuffed now as well, in a puddle of his own vomit. Adele's back was to him, and she was speaking rapidly on the phone.

John drew nearer, relieved to see her standing, speaking, unharmed. He listened as she said, "You're sure? An airfield? Did anyone call him—warn him? No? Perfect. He'll be expecting us. We'll take the Mercedes"

She hung up, turning back to John, her eyes bright with exhilaration. She patted him on the shoulder and winked. "Good job," she said.

John just stared at his girlfriend. "You're a badass, Adele Sharp," he muttered.

"And don't you forget it." Her smile slipped. "BKA says they traced the call. There's a cargo plane on a private airfield at the end of this road. Five miles, tops."

"Think Baris is there?"

She nodded, already moving. "He'll be expecting the Mercedes. We don't want him to take off before we can reach him. Think you're down to drive one of those things?"

John fell quickly into step. "Want the one with the busted windows or the dented door?"

Adele surveyed the scene, she paused to shoot him a look. "What did you do?"

John snorted. "My job. Here—I could use the breeze."

He broke into a jog, hastening towards the car with the bullet holes in the windshield and the shattered passenger window.

Adele followed close behind while the police officers secured the scene.

As John slid into the front seat, checking the keys were in the ignition, he noticed Adele lean out the window, giving a quick side-hug to her father where he'd hurried over, wheezing now like a water buffalo.

"Thanks Dad, for coming. We got them. Thanks for coming."

"Good work, kid," her father said. "You find the boss man?"

Adele nodded quickly, slipping back through the window, daintily, wincing as her vest scraped against glass. "Five miles down the road. Cops are following in the other Mercedes. Mind driving the SUV?"

"You got it."

The Sergeant didn't seem to mind taking orders from his daughter. John had a weird picture where he imagined Claudia, in twenty years, commanding him around a crime scene.

He felt a flush of pride, and his lips turned into a smirk.

"What are you thinking about?" Adele asked, exhaling, and shooting him a look.

"Nothing," John muttered. "Buckle up."

And then he slammed his foot against the gas, ripping back onto the road and spinning in a semi-circle kicking up a cloud of dust.

Adele yelled as he floored the pedal again, tearing down the path, racing towards their would-be rendezvous with a human trafficker.

CHAPTER TWENTY

Adele's heart pounded as they approached a large, metal gate. The doors open, the guardhouse empty.

Adele guessed the guards were currently being shoved into the back of German police cruisers a few miles back up the road. "Slow down, John," she said, "don't alarm him." Ahead, she thought she heard the whir of engines.

Her eyes narrowed. "What's that?"

John grit his teeth and maneuvered through the gate, still speeding. "Plane!" he shouted.

Adele cursed, glancing over her shoulder to track the police cars close behind them, hastening towards the airfield. A long stretch of tarmac indicated the path they should take, ending in an old, run-down two-engine plane, propeller whirring, slowly moving down the runway.

"John!" Adele called, pointing.

"I see it—hang on!"

He floored the vehicle, picking up pace. The concrete around them was a blur as they rushed towards the two blinking red lights on either wing of the plane.

"He's taking off! He must have seen us—dammit!"

"No, he's not," John growled.

They were gaining on the small plane, moving faster, faster, hastening across the asphalt. Adele's stomach threatened her throat, and she gripped the handle above the window until her knuckles nearly popped. Sweat prickled across her wrists—a strange reaction to the heat from the body armor, the stress from the moment and the vent she hadn't thought to turn off in her concentration.

John had both hands gripping the steering wheel, eyes zeroed in on the fleeing plane like some targeting system. Except in this case, they were the missile.

"John—there might be others on the plane!" she screamed. "Careful!"

"What am I," he muttered, still picking up speed, "if not careful."

He suddenly veered the vehicle, trying to clip the back of the plane. He missed.

"Dammit!" he yelled, the wheels squealing, the car jolting as he readjusted.

The miss had cost them valuable time. The plane was well ahead of them now. "I think it's lifting!" Adele shouted. She glimpsed an inch or so of space between the wheels and the tarmac.

"No! Not fast enough yet!" As if in response to his words, the wheels touched back down, and the plane continued to whir forward, faster, faster still.

John, though, was keeping pace, still gaining. Behind them, the cop cars had fanned out, lights whirring. No sense in stealth now—they'd been made.

"Come on," Adele murmured. "Come *on*," she whispered beneath her breath as they tore breakneck across the private airfield.

The front of their Mercedes just barely nudged against the back of the plane. John kept his foot to the floor, slowly nudging the plane.

"Careful!" Adele reminded. "There might be—"

"I know, I know!"

He turned the wheel again, slower this time. As he did, the force of the Mercedes slowly redirected the small biplane.

Adele watched as a small, dark silhouette in the pilot's seat slammed a hand against the glass window in fury as he was forced to redirect.

John was moving slowly enough that the plane didn't topple, but forcefully enough that it was now losing speed in order to turn and facing in the wrong direction.

John chuckled, muttering, "Fly over that."

Adele glanced through the window, her heart still pattering, and she realized what Renee had done. A water tower in the distance as well as elevated terrain would make a take-off treacherous. The plane would have to turn completely around to get a clear path off the airstrip. Now, it was heading towards the weeds.

The pilot was no longer slamming the glass but had resumed his grip on the controls, readjusting the plane. The angry red lights behind the aircraft continued to blink like a demon's eyes, staring at the encroaching law enforcement vehicles.

Adele's breath came quickly, her heart still fluttering.

Then, the plane began to slow.

"Yes!" she shouted.

John's lips were tight again, his eyes narrowed as he stared towards the pilot and a second figure sitting next to him, visible through the glass.

The plane continued to slow and finally came to a full stop on the edge of the runway, the nose dipping over a cluster of towering weeds. The propeller slowly whined to a stop.

John sent their vehicle into a skid, slamming on the breaks and rotating their vehicle to provide cover. The moment he put the Mercedes in park, Adele and John burst from the compartment, swinging open their doors, guns jammed through the windows, using the doors as cover.

Sirens blared behind them. More men and women with guns arrived at the scene. More shouting.

After a few moments, the cockpit's doors opened, rising up like the wings of some bird. Two men jutted their hands out at the sky. The pilot was a small, mousy man and he kept glancing nervously towards the figure sitting next to him.

This second man drew Adele's attention. She frowned in the direction of this passenger, her gun trained.

"Get out!" she was shouting. "Turn off the plane and get out with your hands up!"

The pilot wasted no time in doing so. He exited the front seat but was soon followed. Not by the passenger, but by two young women, both with streaked mascara and small carry-on luggage items they clutched tightly to their chests.

They stumbled on the tarmac, both wearing high heels.

"Hands in the air!" the German cops shouted. "Hands up!"

The women dropped their luggage, sending their palms skyward, shaking in terror like leaves in a gale.

Cops rushed forward, securing the three figures. The pilot was cuffed. The two women were aided towards the back of a cruiser— likely to wait for an ambulance.

But Adele's gaze turned back towards the passenger side of the plane.

Lazily, like a cat stretching in sunlight, this final figure slipped from the side seat and hit the tarmac. He turned slowly, glancing around, his hands still raised.

"Get down!" Adele called, along with a choir of other shouting voices. At the same time, she quickly examined the man in question. No visible firearm. No weapon of any kind.

He looked as if he'd just been out for a stroll in the woods. He even paused to stretch, crossing one arm over his chest and pulling it tight with his off hand. He yawned briefly, giving a sleepy little shake of his head, and then raised his wrists. He looked from one cop to the other, as if searching for something. Slowly, he rounded on Adele, and his eyes flickered. He flashed a smile, mostly white, but a glint of gold in the left side of his mouth.

He extended his arms towards her, wrists up, and quirked an eyebrow. Other figures were moving, rushing towards him, but even as they hastened forward, he didn't lift his gaze from Adele. He winked as a couple of cops reached him, cuffs flying. They pushed him to his knees and interlocked his arms behind his back.

Through it all, his gaze never left Adele.

She stared back, frowning at the man.

He looked like a banker or an office worker. A neat haircut. Average height. Olive complexion. And he also looked entirely at ease, as if this were no more than a little jaunt down south for a quick vacation.

As the cops pushed him back to his feet, cuffed now, and herded him towards a waiting police car, the man finally looked away from Adele, a faint smile curling his lips.

John nudged Adele from the side. The big man was breathing heavily but looked a bit like a lost puppy now that the action had ended. If anything, he looked mildly disappointed he hadn't been allowed to shoot anyone.

"Good job," Adele said, patting her partner on the arm.

"You too. What now?"

"Now... Now I think we talk to that golden-toothed crocodile over there."

"The girls?"

Adele glanced towards where the two women were being spoken to by a female officer.

She sighed. "Keep them in custody until we sort this all out. Leave it to the locals, though—we're here for one thing only."

"Right," John said. "Our victims... Think he could be the killer?"

"It's possible. He was connected to one of our victims. Hell—look at what he pulled back there. Clearly these women are little more than commodities to him. Maybe some of them weren't able to pay his fees. He asked for half of everything they made."

"Shit. That's almost as bad as the government."

"We *are* the government, John."

"A truly tragic tale." John sighed. "Well, can't hurt to speak to him on the way to the precint. Maybe he'll be more willing to talk while in motion."

Adele was already in motion, marching towards the police cruiser where the man with the golden tooth had been placed.

CHAPTER TWENTY ONE

Adele could smell the man's aftershave from the front seat. The moment she slid into the vehicle, her nose twitched at the pungent odor. Perhaps that was why the driver's side door had been left open. Adele reached across the divide, grabbed the door handle and swung it shut with a quiet *click*. She stared through the windshield for a moment, refusing to acknowledge their suspect at first. Agent Renee was watching from where he leaned against the hood of the nearest car. For the moment, though, he kept at a distance, allowing Adele her space.

She inhaled slowly, calming her nerves. She then glanced in the rearview mirror.

"Baris?" she said.

He met her gaze, his eyes carrying that same haughty look from earlier. "I saw you on camera," he replied. "If I hadn't been distracted by that fool pilot, I would've seen you sooner."

"So you are Baris?"

He shrugged. "I didn't do anything wrong."

"I recognize your voice. And if you didn't do anything wrong, why were you trying to flee?"

He raised his hands, rattling his handcuffs. "A misunderstanding."

She didn't like the way he spoke. Too at ease. Too comfortable.

"I have you on human trafficking."

"Trafficking?" He snorted. "Smuggling. Huge difference. Much lower sentences."

Adele turned now, facing him head on. "Smuggling?"

He flashed a smile, revealing a glimpse of gold in the corner of his mouth. "I'm a friend to these women," he said simply. "You said you were at which club?"

Adele doubted he had forgotten. Probably a trick question to try and help narrow down who had given her his number. She didn't answer. Instead, she said, "You victimize these women. Fifty-percent—that's a joke."

He snorted, shaking his head. "It's business. I feed them. Clothe them. Fly them. Place them. And I keep them safe."

"I had a taste of that safety on the road back there," Adele said sarcastically.

For the first time, the man looked irritated. But not at her. "Did one of them cause you trouble?"

"You could say that. Right before I kneed him in the crotch."

Baris sighed, muttering something in a language she didn't understand. "New hires. I must apologize, profusely," he said, quickly, his tone changing. "A business is only as good as its reputation. I hope you know I would've compensated you for any damage."

Adele just watched him. He was a mass of contradictions. His tone almost sounded genuine when apologizing. The thought of anyone harming his business reputation genuinely seemed to bother him. "These women are prostitutes. You traffic them from one country to another."

"These women are victims. Who need my help. Besides, what they do should be legal anyway."

"It is legal in Germany, in parts, with registration," she added. "So how come you have those two women in that plane with you?"

He snorted. "Unlicensed. None of my business anyway. They wanted a ride, and I agreed. We met on terms, and everything was aboveboard. They were safe too. Ask them. Ask them if anyone hurt them. That's not how I run my operation."

"So you admit it's an operation?"

"I'm just trying to make you see a little bit of sense," he said. "You went to a lot of effort to tackle one of the good guys." He flashed another smile.

CHAPTER TWENTY TWO

Adele knew he meant his comments to be disarming, but they were unsettling. "That's how you see yourself?" he asked. "One of the good guys?"

"What's this about, really? German authorities have known about me in the past. No one's gone to such efforts. I don't hurt anyone. I even help the economy. I remove women who are breaking the law, while keeping them safe, and take them back to their home countries, or somewhere more amenable to their line of work."

Adele just stared at him. She hadn't heard this tactic before. Playing the victim as a trafficker. Acting like some sort of good Samaritan. If anything, he almost seemed to believe his own words. His tone had a note of authenticity to it that sent shivers up her spine. She wasn't sure she liked the way he was looking at her, as if seeing her as the bad guy.

"Why are you doing this?" he said. "Why *really*?"

"You come across quite high and mighty for a man in your line of work," she said, avoiding the question and attempting to rattle him again.

He snorted, shaking his head. "I treat them well. I don't kidnap anyone. There are no victims." He pivoted. "What's your name? I don't forget a name. And I definitely don't forget a face."

A faint shiver prickled up Adele's spine. Her eyes narrowed at the sensation. "You don't forget a name?" she said. "All right. I have some names. Sasha De Guyne. She went by Silver. Heard of her?"

The man flinched. He swallowed. "What is this really about?"

"Monique Sargant," she said, more firmly. "That's the name I gave you on the phone. You recognized it."

"Monique. Of course. Tall, blonde. Nice legs. Like I said, I remember my clients. She is a good girl."

Adele noted the present tense. The man was rattled and yet he spoke as if she were still alive. Was he just that good? Or maybe he didn't know...

"They're both dead," Adele said simply. "Sasha and Monique. Dead."

He gaped at her. His smug expression melted. His jaw unhinged. Quickly, he tried to collect himself, looking out the window and clearing his throat. Once he had settled, he looked back at her, straight postured, pretending he hadn't cracked. "That's horrible to hear," he said simply. "How?"

"I was hoping you would tell me." She let the words themselves carry the weight of their meaning.

His lip tucked under his golden tooth as he nibbled. "Shit. Now I see. You think I killed them."

"Did you?"

"Hell no. Why would I? They never missed a payment."

"Can you prove that?"

"You wish. I'm not showing you my financials."

"We'll find out soon enough."

He muttered, "Good luck." His shoulders hunched now. In that suit of his he didn't look nearly so impressive. If anything, now he looked mad.

"You're saying you didn't even know about their deaths?"

"Of course not! Hell, I wouldn't have been taking new girls if I had. I would've gotten out of town, quick. I was in Lithuania last week. Far fewer regulations. I certainly wasn't going to be around a murder rap."

Adele felt a flicker of unease. "Lithuania?"

"It's a country. Look at a map."

"I know what it is. Why were you there?"

He shot her a cagey look. "Business."

"Do you have proof you were there?"

"Why would I want to prove that?"

"Do you?"

"Plane tickets. Hotel bills. Hell, check my right pocket, I still have the phone I activated while there. Different area code and everything."

Adele made a mental note to get an officer to do just that. Inwardly, her mind was whirring. He had admitted to knowing both victims. Why would he have done that if he had known they were dead? Far more likely he *hadn't* known. Hadn't thought it would tie him up in a murder beat. But that meant he wasn't involved. Or at the very least he didn't know about the murders.

Plus, if his phone did confirm he was in Lithuania, he couldn't have been in Amsterdam strangling Sasha.

Adele let out a hissing sigh. "They're taking you in for further questioning," she said.

"I'll be out in a month. Want some advice?" he said raising an eyebrow.

She snorted. "On the case? From you?"

"Couldn't hurt. You missed big. Thinking it's me means you don't know who it is. Means you're grasping at straws."

"Or I got exactly who I was fishing for," she retorted.

He waved away the objection.

"If you thought that was true, you wouldn't still be sitting there. I'd be back at the precinct, being booked."

"That's gonna happen," Adele retorted.

"Victimless crime," he replied.

Adele wasn't sure what to think of this. He seemed confident that he was telling the truth. He saw himself as some sort of liberator. The women he helped smuggle recommended him to others. Otherwise, that older woman back at the German brothel would not have kept his business card. Something about his reputation must've been useful. But also, with men like this, in situations like these, there were often unseen, hidden costs that only materialized later.

Still, her instincts were screaming. This business of being out of the country, combined with the present tense use of the victim who'd been killed in Amsterdam, not to mention the look on his face when she had told him... She was having serious doubts. Now that he had confirmed he'd been involved smuggling the fake Frenchwoman, Adele wasn't sure where that led her.

She didn't normally make a habit of taking hints from criminals. But he seemed genuinely concerned when she'd told him previous clients of his had died.

"See, the problem here," Baris said, giving her a significant look, "is you're trying to blame someone who was helping these women."

"So you say. That's what you call advice?"

"Maybe you should focus on those people who had something invested. Something they could lose," he said, glancing at his hands, his fingers tapping against each other.

"What does that mean?"

"It means you only kill for three reasons."

Adele looked at him. "Money, sex, and power."

He tapped his nose and pointed at her. "Workers don't have power and they provide sex. Why would you kill something that gives you what you want? But money? Where they're involved, things can get tricky." He raised his hands to show his cuffs. "Exhibit A," he muttered.

Adele leaned back, glancing in the rearview mirror now instead of looking at him straight on.

"Just sit still, sir," she said. "You'll be processed soon."

Then, she pushed out of the car, stepping back onto the small airfield. Other vehicles were now pulling away as cops left the scene. John was waiting by the hood of an SUV. Her father was nowhere to be seen.

She approached Renee, frowning. "Seen my dad?"

John grunted. "He went back in the car with the man you beat up."

Adele glanced back down the road.

"I think he wanted a couple of words with the guy."

Adele sighed, shaking her head. Hot and cold. Her relationship with her father was a wonderful mystery. Now, though, she was troubled.

"Did he bite?" John said.

Adele shot a look back towards the police car and its occupant. He was still watching her, through the glass.

She looked towards John and replied quietly, "I don't think it's him. He has an alibi. Not verified. But I don't think it's him."

"So what now?"

"Obviously the killer is after a very specific type of girl with a specific appearance. Belgian girls. But why?"

"Just a preference?" John guessed.

"It must be more than that. He targeted these particular girls. That means he knew them. Or at least knew of them."

"So he knew the girls. Maybe he was a regular, someone we just weren't able to place. Maybe he dressed different when he visited them. Maybe he came so irregularly no one noticed."

"Or maybe," Adele said, quietly, "they weren't killed because of who they were. But rather because of what they knew."

She shot another look back towards the car. She didn't like to think that a trafficker had gotten in her head. But he made sense. What if this was about money? Not money the girls would earn, but money someone else could *lose*. How would killing a prostitute save money? Unless they knew something. Unless the person who had killed them had a lot to cover.

"What are you thinking?"

"I'm thinking maybe our killer had a previous relationship with these women. And maybe, for some reason, some life change, something, that relationship had to be terminated."

"Permanently," John said.

"Exactly. Nothing like an illicit sex life to damage your reputation, right? If this person was frequenting brothels, hookers, maybe he had to just tidy things up."

"So you think the killer might've targeted these women so no one else would find out he had visited them? A new wife? Something...

business related? It's speculation, Adele."

"I know. But it makes sense. Besides, we don't have anything else. It wasn't Baris. I'd bet anything. He didn't even know they were dead."

"Maybe he's a psychopath. Lying through his teeth."

"Maybe," Adele said, hesitantly. "We'll know soon enough. I'm leaving a note for the detectives to go through his phone. Check his financials. If he was in Lithuania, then he didn't do it. He couldn't have been in Amsterdam at the same time."

"Maybe he hired someone."

"To kill a prostitute? Why?"

"Business? I don't know."

"Why kill someone who is making you money?" Adele felt torn. The theory could work. If she stretched it. But on the other hand, her instincts told her Baris was innocent of the murders. He had seemed genuinely surprised, disappointed. He hadn't faked grief but had seemed upset at the prospect of his business reputation being tarnished. Which left her with very few options.

She exhaled slowly, and then said, "I want to go to Monique's apartment. Maybe she has something there. If this guy has a history with her, maybe I can find out how."

John paused, studying her, but then didn't protest. He gave a brief nod. "Sounds good. I'll drive."

CHAPTER TWENTY THREE

Adele paused outside the yellow apartment door, her knuckles brushing the metal surface. She inhaled slowly, wondering if perhaps she ought to have brought John with her. But no—the big Frenchman might just scare Monique's roommate.

Adele adjusted her sleeves, raised her hand again and knocked. She then stepped back, turned sideways, presenting as non-threatening a silhouette as possible, and waited politely.

A few seconds passed and she heard the sound of lethargic footfalls.

As Adele listened to the approaching footsteps, her phone buzzed. She glanced at the device to find a text message from Agent Renee.

The text simply read: *your dad is here.*

Great. Adele sighed. John was back at the precinct, where she had insisted that he stay while she dealt with this particular interview. Officially, she didn't want the large man to scare away the victim's roommate. Unofficially, Adele didn't trust John around prostitutes. Or, more accurately, she didn't trust herself around John when women kept shooting him sidelong glances or fluttering their eyelashes or trying to touch his arms. She was sick of it. Having him as backup while chasing down a trafficker was one thing, but interviewing a single woman in an apartment? She could do that on her own.

She pocketed her phone and turned to face the door.

The door opened, accompanying the sound of a rattling chain.

"Yes?" came a gruff voice. The voice didn't quite match the speaker. The woman in the door was quite attractive with round, pleasant cheeks and bright eyes. Her hair though, was a bird's nest. She looked like she had just gotten up from a nap, stifling a yawn as she stared suspiciously through the crack in her apartment door. Adele smiled politely and nodded in greeting. "My name is Agent Sharp, with Interpol. I was wondering if I could speak to you about your roommate."

The woman in the door didn't speak. She just frowned, looking Adele up and down.

Hastily, Adele pulled out her identification, flashing it.

The woman in the door visibly relaxed; the door shut, the chain rattled as it was unhooked, and then the door opened again. The woman said, "Sorry. Sometimes clients track us down. You can never be too careful."

Adele nodded politely. She peered past the beautiful woman with the bird's nest hair, her eyes darting around the living room with clothing scattered over a couch, towards the kitchen table covered in a pile of books being organized into rows.

The woman shrugged sheepishly, glancing back, "Sorry, you caught me at a bit of a bad time. I'm going through Monique's things."

Adele shook her head. "No problem. That's why I'm here. Do you mind if I come in?"

Monique's roommate hesitated nervously. She glanced back towards Adele's hand that had replaced the ID, and then sighed, her disheveled bangs puffing like willow leaves, and she turned, gesturing for Adele to join her once again in the room.

Adele followed at a respectful distance. She said, "I don't want to be in your hair. Mind showing me to Monique's room?"

The roommate sidestepped, moving behind the couch. She didn't seem to like having Adele walk behind her; she kept shifting uncomfortably. Adele had seen the same sort of cautious behavior in trauma survivors. The roommate gestured with one hand down the hall. "Second room," she said.

Adele flashed a grateful smile and moved towards the indicated space. The only one with the door open. Her curiosity dragged her gaze to a couple of the sealed rooms, and she wondered if the roommate had closed them before answering the knock on the apartment door. Strange. Clearly, the woman was distrusting of strangers. If she shared Monique's line of work, this wasn't surprising.

Adele glanced around the third victim's bedroom. Neat, tidy. A couple of posters of famous singers on the wall. A picture of a bucolic, mountainside farm painted with acrylic over a writing desk. An old-fashioned record player sat by the bed with a collection of vinyl in a cubbyhole just beneath it. Currently, the album art of the record inside the player was of a musician Adele had never heard of. *Klaus Wunderlich.*

She turned, examining the single bed. The woman didn't take her work home.

At the foot of the bed, she spotted a dresser, and Adele moved towards this, pulling at the top drawers.

In one, she found a stack of money. At least the roommate was an honest person. She hadn't stolen from her deceased friend.

Adele found a sock drawer, an underwear drawer, and a drawer filled with coat hangers for some reason.

She turned, glancing at the closet. This was open too. And like the rest of the room, it was kept neat and organized. Everything on hooks and hangers. Adele spotted a guitar case, and she opened this, looking inside. There was no guitar, but there were a couple of baggies with pills in them.

Ecstasy? Vicodin? She would have to see if John knew. She took a picture of the pills, but decided they weren't worth taking for the moment. Nothing about the murders suggested they were drug related.

She turned away, and her eyes moved from the record player, this time, to a small wooden dish on a window ledge behind the nightstand.

Something glinted, catching her eye.

Adele frowned, sidling around the bed once more. She carefully moved the record player. No dust, she noticed, suggesting it was common practice to relocate the thing.

There, beneath the blinds, sheltered out of sight from the record player except for the very edge, was a wooden dish filled with trinkets.

Adele pulled the blinds, and peered into the dish, frowning.

There was a heart locket, a small statue of a porcelain angel, a couple of cards, a pack of chocolates, half-empty, and there, the object that had glinted: a diamond pendant.

Adele stared, leaning in. She didn't touch anything but frowned at the pendant. "Excuse me?" She called out, projecting back towards the hall.

There was another pause, and then the same lethargic footsteps from earlier. The roommate appeared in the doorway.

Adele pointed to the wooden dish filled with trinkets. "What are these?"

"I don't know."

Adele turned now. "I'm so sorry, I don't think I caught your name."

Her eyes darted, the woman swallowed, brushing hair behind an ear. "Gloria."

Adele had already looked up the woman's name before coming. It wasn't Gloria. But she wasn't here for the roommate. "Gloria," she said, without missing a beat, "is there anything you can tell me about your roommate? Anyone she might have been involved with?"

The roommate shifted uncomfortably, rubbing at her arm.

Adele smiled in a reassuring manner. "If I didn't know better, I would guess those items are little gifts. Did clients give them to her?"

The woman in the door looked downright uncomfortable now. "I don't know anything. I wasn't involved. I got out of the business a couple of months ago. Before all of this."

"You seem like a good friend."

"I'm very tired. I don't know anything."

"I'm not trying to cause you trouble," Adele said, gently. "I'm trying to find who killed Monique—anything you know could help find the man who did this and also protect the next woman. Like your roommate." Adele went quiet, allowing the words to linger a moment before she asked again "Are you sure you don't know anything about those items?"

The woman shrugged, still gripping her arm tightly with her other hand. "I guess you could be right. Probably from clients."

"Did Monique ever talk about her clients?"

A brief moment of hesitation. A look of sheer terror, then a swallow and a sidelong glance. Gloria refused to meet Adele's gaze. "No," she said in a small voice.

"Nothing at all?"

"Nothing."

Adele turned, picking out the diamond pendant from the dish, using the edges of her fingers on the very tip of the clasp, to avoid contaminating any fingerprints on the face. "This looks expensive. You're sure you don't know who sent this to her?"

The look of terror returned. Gloria shot a panicked look from the pendant to Adele. "I don't know anything. Please. These are dangerous people. I just want to get out of here. I'm moving back with my parents. Can you leave? I don't know."

Adele let out a faint sigh. "Dangerous people? What sort of dangerous people?"

"I *don't* know." Gloria was beginning to grow agitated. She shook her head violently. "If I tell you things, I could end up just like Monique. It's why I left the work. It doesn't let you leave without scars!" She pulled down the edge of her shirt, showing her shoulder and collarbone. Adele stared at small pock marks of scarred skin

Gloria's eyes widened as she whispered, "He seemed so nice. And then he put his cigarette out in me six times before the bouncer came and took him away. They barely even fined him—no prison time. I'm forgettable. No one cares. And anything you say might lead back to me." She adjusted her shirt again, crossing her arms defiantly. She glared. "Now please, take what you want, then go."

Adele felt a lance of grief. In her heart and mind, she hadn't been taking it very easy on women in this profession. Now, though, staring at Gloria, all she felt was an overwhelming surge of compassion. She couldn't imagine living a life like that. The scar marks on her shoulder from cigarette burns alone made Adele's blood boil. The thought of someone getting away with something like that made her furious. The same fury welled inside her. Her tone shook, her voice unsteady but passionate as she said, "I swear to you this will not come back to you. I will protect you. I will not mention your name. I'm trying to stop someone who killed your friend. This same sort of person who did that to your shoulder. It's not your fault. At all. But sometimes the reason people like this get away is because everyone keeps their lips sealed. And I get it. Really. Sometimes it can feel like no one takes you seriously. But I will protect your identity. And I will find the guy who did this to Monique, and put him away forever. Please. Help me. Anything you know. Whisper it. I won't tell a soul. I just need to know the information so I can use it. Who gave her this pendant? Why would someone give a prostitute something this valuable?"

Gloria shifted uncomfortably, mumbled something beneath her breath, her fingers twitching towards the collar of her shirt, wincing as if from some ghost pain of a long-healed wound; then, in a small voice, she said, "You need to leave."

Adele let out a faint sigh; she knew she could take Gloria downtown for questioning. Gloria was scared. That much was clear. Partially, Adele guessed, due to her own trauma and experiences in the same line of work. Adele didn't want to make her life more miserable. But she also needed information.

She placed the diamond trinket back in the wooden bowl and took a picture of it on her phone. Then said, with a breath, "I'll show myself out."

She moved past the roommate, hands in her pockets, thinking desperately.

The roommate was clearly hiding something. Did Adele want to strongarm her? She was sick of that tactic. Sick of forcing people to put themselves in harm's way for the greater good.

Adele approached the front door, considering any angle. Maybe she could take Gloria on as a CI and offer her a fee for the information. That might work. But it would lead to a paper trail. She had just told the woman, given her word, that she wouldn't drag her name into this.

Adele sighed, opening the door and stepping out into the hallway, still conflicted.

"Scholz," came a small voice from down the hall.

Adele turned sharply, staring towards where Gloria stood in the doorway.

"What was that?"

"Scholz," she said, more insistently. "Mikhail Scholz," she said a final time. "That's who gave her the pendant. The record player. The money you found in the cabinet. And if you saw those pills in the guitar case—also from him. A very big spender, and a very dangerous man. Now you promised. He can't know I told you."

"I swear it. Thank you. Mikhail Scholz. He was a regular client of Monique's?"

"Not just regular. Sometimes her only client. He would pay for months at a time for her not to sleep with anyone else. Tons of money. More than I ever earned in the business. He was a white whale. But that much money comes with strings." She shrugged, shaking her head. "Do you think he had anything to do with her death?"

"By your tone it sounds like *you* think he might have."

A panicked look crossed Gloria's face again. She shook her head. "I never said that. I *never* said that. I will not stand as a witness. Whatever you do, I never said anything. You promised."

Adele held up her hands. "I promised. It's okay. You have my word. Thank you."

Gloria gave a quick nod. Then she closed the door. She stood in the hallway for a moment, exhaling slowly.

It felt nice that she been given the information without having to resort to some bully tactic. Sometimes, she felt like the job was so urgent, such high stakes, that along the way they bulldozed citizens who couldn't take care of themselves.

That was always the cost of a power dynamic. The more powerful the person, the easier it was to cross boundaries without even realizing it.

Mikhail Scholz. By the sound of things, another very powerful person.

Who had the most to lose?

That was what Baris had said. That was what Adele was now thinking. The sort of man who could buy record players, pay for a high-end prostitute months at a time, buy diamond pendants. That was also the sort of man who had a lot to lose.

She turned, walking quickly back around the banister and hurrying down the stairs. She pulled her phone from her pocket, calling Agent Renee.

"John, hang on. Yes, I'm coming back. I want you to look up a name for me: Mikhail Scholz. Yeah, I think he's involved. Just look it up. Tell me what you find."

She hung up and moved hurriedly back out the front door of the apartment towards where she had parked her borrowed car.

CHAPTER TWENTY FOUR

Adele pulled into the parking lot outside the large, ten-story, glass and concrete building. A new construction, judging by the state of the white paint, and bold, blue block letters over the door that simply read, *Scholz Industries.*

Ahead, she spotted Agent Renee sitting in the driver's seat of an SUV. Her father reclined next to him. Adele frowned. She turned off the engine, pushed out of her car and hastened towards the idling automobile.

John glanced in the side mirror, noted her, and swung open the door. The Sergeant hit the pavement a step behind, watching his daughter approach.

Adele's gaze bounced between the two of them. "This is a surprise," she said, slowly, frowning from one to the other.

"He wouldn't take no for an answer," John replied gruffly, shooting a dirty glance towards the Sergeant.

Adele bit her lip. "I'm not sure you should be here, Dad."

Joseph Sharp waved away her protest. "I drove two hours to help," he said simply. "I almost had to listen over the radio as three men nearly killed you. I'm coming."

Adele pointed at the sidewalk. "In fact, you're already here." She turned her look of frustration back towards John. "You couldn't have just driven away?"

Renee sighed, massaging the bridge of his nose. "He's quick. Like an otter."

The Sergeant looked quite pleased at this comparison.

Adele didn't have the mental capacity to deal with this right now. Her father was a policeman. He was technically allowed to participate in cases. But that didn't mean it wasn't uncomfortable for her. Still, things were still mending between them. She didn't want to put her foot down too hard and risk chasing him away. Besides, the rich and powerful were dangerous, but not in the same way a biker gang or a couple of hoodlums were. Scholz wouldn't just start shooting. He was the sort to use lawyers or contractors to do his dirty work.

She turned towards John. "You're sure about that lead you had on the ownership of the company?"

John nodded. "Double checked. His wife owns the place; he's only the CEO. Salaried. Probably some equity stake, but not much."

Adele gave a satisfied nod, her expression grim. "The perfect reason to try and keep an illicit affair under wraps, right?"

John turned also, peering up at the large structure standing out against the darkening skies. "With his wife as the owner, she could fire him, and he would lose everything. You think Monique was trying to talk? Or maybe Scholz was up to something that he thought he could keep under wraps but got cold feet?"

"Did you see the flight records I sent you?"

John nodded. "He was in Amsterdam last week."

Adele's eyes narrowed. "Exactly."

She marched up the sidewalk, moving towards the large, rotating glass door in the lobby of the large office building.

A few employees were moving in and out. Evening had fallen, and people were heading home for the night. Cars started in the parking lot; behind them half the spaces were empty. But with a quick estimate, Adele guessed the capacity of the lots was at least five hundred.

No small company.

Her father waddled behind the two of them as John and Adele pushed through the rotating glass door into the lobby

A receptionist behind an exceptionally long counter looked up, smiling as they approached. The woman had bright, white teeth, and skin to match. Her eyes creased, and she beamed. "Welcome to Scholz industries," she said happily. "How can I help you?"

"We need to speak with the boss," Adele said simply.

The receptionist's smile slipped. "Do you have an appointment?"

John, who couldn't understand German, still knew the routine. And together, Renee and Adele slapped their identifications on the counter in synchronization.

"That's my appointment," Adele said. "Top floor? He seems like a top floor type of guy. Tell him we're coming. Or don't."

She pocketed her ID, and turned, marching towards the nearest elevator. She could still hear that note of fear in Gloria's voice. Could still see the way the prostitutes had been choked to death.

Scholz had been in Amsterdam during the time of the murders. He'd come back to Germany on a flight just in time to kill Monique. His wife owned the company. Which gave him substantial reason to cover his behavior. On top of that, Adele had looked up pictures of the woman on the company website. Tall, pale-haired, pretty.

Mrs. Scholz, the owner, resembled the three dead prostitutes.

Adele felt a surge of pride at Gloria's courage to tell Adele what she knew. People like this thought they could buy everything. It was why she had noticed the diamond pendant. Money could open lips, seal them. It could open hands and close them. It would open doors and shut them, but money could only go so far. And the fear of losing it could push a soul to do irregular things.

Adele's eyes narrowed, and she jammed her thumb against the elevator button one too many times. John reached out, touching her wrist and gently lowering it.

"Calm down," he whispered beneath his breath.

Adele's father didn't say anything but stood behind them in his blue uniform, his weapon holstered, his fingers looped through his belt. He had a look of ease, but Adele could feel her own heart pounding rapidly. Places like this, people with this much influence, this much power, gave her the creeps.

The elevator dinged, reaching the bottom floor, and the three of them shuffled in. The last glimpse she had of the lobby was the receptionist's panicked look, a phone cradled against her cheek as she rapidly warned the top floor about the incoming agents.

***

The elevator doors opened to reveal a row of potted plants. No flowers, just large green leaves. The sort of leaves one might use for camouflage. But there would be no hiding here. Adele took one look at the top floor, and her eyes landed on the largest doors. "Bingo," she said, pointing.

She didn't wait for John or her father but stepped off the elevator and marched across the close-cut gray carpet, making a beeline towards these double doors. From within, she heard voices. Adele's eyes narrowed, some of the same anger she'd felt back at the third victim's apartment now rising within her. In her mind, she rehearsed what they knew. Scholz had been connected to Monique. He had just come back from Amsterdam. He'd spent a lot of money on a prostitute. His wife owned the company. A slam dunk. Motive, means, opportunity.

Who stood to lose the most?

She barged into the office, deciding to play this aggressively. Putting a man like Scholz on his back foot was important. The sooner he got to calling lawyers and favors, the harder it would be to peg him.

As she pushed into the office, she was confronted by more green, potted plants. A couple of these boasted cactuses. One was of a miniature tree with strange, banana-shaped leaves. An enormous desk sat against the glass wall, overlooking the city like a king might gaze upon his realm.

A man behind the desk looked up, startled, a phone held in one hand. But he wasn't alone. A tall woman, with pale hair and a neat bun was standing by the desk; the woman frowned towards the door but looked less rattled.

"You can't be in here!" the man called.

Adele watched as he hastily hung up the phone and began adjusting some of the papers on his desk as if somehow organization might save him.

"Are you Scholz?" Adele demanded.

The man shifted uncomfortably in a large, black, leather desk chair. One of the wheels squeaked when he moved.

"I'm the CEO," he said, "and who are you?"

The woman pressed a button on the corded phone. "Security!" she said.

Her eyes darted past Adele towards John and the Sergeant. She tensed, frowning.

"I'm sure there's no need for security," said Mr. Scholz waving his hand, and flashing an uneasy smile. He pushed to his feet, and his desk chair squeaked again. Undoubtedly, he was the one who had fielded the call from reception. He knew they were law enforcement. A million-dollar counterfeit smile spread across his cheeks. He beamed from Adele to John and back. He gave a little shrug, and said, "How can I help you?"

"I have some questions for you," Adele said without missing a beat. She glanced towards the woman. "Probably best if we speak alone."

"Yes, of course," Scholz said quickly, still forcing that horrible grin of his. "Maybe just a few minutes."

But his wife cut him off. "I own this company. I'll stay."

"Mrs. Scholz?" Adele asked.

The woman's eyes narrowed, and she crossed her forearms over a neat, pressed suit. "What is this about? And who are you?"

John had reached Adele's side, identification raised. "DGSI," he said, "we're working with Interpol."

"I see." Her look of rank disapproval shifted now, moving from the three figures who had barged into the office, landing squarely on her squirming husband.

"I really think this would be done better in private," Adele said, allowing a warning note to creep into her voice.

The man tried to speak, but his wife cut in again. "I'll stay. I insist."

Mr. Scholz sunk into his seat, his face pale.

Adele shrugged. Not that she minded. She'd tried twice. No one could accuse her of being unprofessional now. Besides, sometimes it was fun to watch a shark sink beneath the shadow of a larger predator. She stared at Mr. Scholz, iron in her gaze. "Did you know Monique?"

The man blinked. "Who?" he said quickly.

"She was a prostitute," Adele replied, her tone betraying no emotion. "And she was killed less than two days ago. We have reason to believe you knew her."

Now his pale face had gone ghostly. He slumped in his chair but shook his head. The view behind him didn't look so spectacular now. "No," he said hurriedly. "I've never heard of her. You must've made a mistake. Maybe if we go down to the station... I'll call my lawyer."

Adele ignored this and pressed, "Were you in Amsterdam recently?"

He hesitated, his eyes shifting. His wife would know he had been. Adele could see the wheels moving in his mind. At last, he shrugged. "Is that a crime?"

"No. But we had two prostitutes killed in Amsterdam. They looked a lot like Monique. A lot like your wife," Adele said, glancing towards Mrs. Scholz again.

"How dare you!" Mr. Scholz exclaimed, but his heart wasn't in it. The words sounded wooden, hollow. He also seemed to be holding back tears. His eyes were red, his breath coming quickly. Tears of shame? Guilt? Anger?

His hands gripped the armrests tightly, fingers curled like claws.

"Sir, I have to advise you, you don't want to lie to law enforcement."

"I'm not lying," he snapped. "I didn't kill anyone. I don't know these women."

Adele's gaze shifted towards the owner of Scholz industries. A cold, unblinking expression. Adele said, "You knew?"

She phrased it as a question, but she didn't need an answer.

Still, Mrs. Scholz provided one anyway. "It's all right Mikhail, you can tell the truth. I knew about Monique. I've known for months now." That same dispassionate tone. "It was going to come up in your next job review," she said, her countenance like a closed tomb.

Her husband squeaked; this time it wasn't the chair. He stared up at his wife, mouth unhinged. "I don't know what they're talking about! It's a lie. A fabrication. Our enemies—they're trying to divide us!"

Mrs. Scholz smiled now and reached down, patting his cheek. "Of course, dear," she said in a sickly, sweet tone. "That's why I found $10,000 receipts for hotel rooms, catering, and what was the last one, oh, yes, a *business* dinner."

She patted his face, a little bit harder this time. She lowered her hand. "I've known, Mikhail. I suppose now is as good a time to bring it up." She turned to face the agents. "My husband did know this whore. In Germany. I've been keeping an eye on her and him. But he didn't visit any brothels in Amsterdam."

Adele stared. "How can you be sure?"

"Because, dear, I was with him on the business trip." She glared. "Every moment of every day. We had meetings fourteen hours a day. Made more money in a single trip than I have in this country's horrid economy. Plus, I've been keeping track of every financial transaction he's made over the last six months."

Her husband was staring at his wife now, stunned. She gave a little clucking sound. "Normally you have so much to say, Mikhail."

Adele glanced back at the CEO. The tears were now trickling down the inside of his cheek. He wasn't able to hold them back. His mouth opened and closed, and he gave a frantic shake of his head. "You knew?" He said in a breathy voice. "How did you know?"

"You're not as sly as you think you are. I didn't mind. Not while it didn't distract you from your work. The big purchases," she said, firmly, "will be taken from your next paycheck. I hope you understand."

Everything from Mrs. Scholz was cold, calculated, firm. She didn't seem upset. She didn't seem sad. She just sounded disappointed that it had come out like this. But another part of her seemed to be relishing the conversation. There was a crocodile glint in her eyes.

Adele stared at Mikhail. He was crying. His head hanging in his hands now. His shoulders shook with sobs. His wife leaned in, giving him a quick side squeeze of a hug. It wasn't an affectionate gesture. More like a robot going through motions. This only caused her husband to begin to weep.

John cleared his throat uncomfortably. Adele just watched, trying to piece it all together.

If the wife was telling the truth, then neither of them would have been able to get away in Amsterdam to do anything. They would have to check those financial statements. Why was Mr. Scholz weeping, though?

As if this thought prompted his response, he hiccupped, loosed a long, wilting sigh, then said, sniffling, "I loved her. I *loved* her! But I never would leave you for her. She wanted me to. But I never did. I would never leave you."

Mrs. Scholz patted her husband's head like a doting mother tending to a child. "I know."

"But I can't help what I love. I didn't even know she was dead," he said, breaking into another round of weeping. The tears he'd been trying to hold back to save face now burst through the floodgates.

Adele could feel her discomfort rising.

Was Mr. Scholz acting—was Mrs. Scholz in on it? What if this was all one big pretense?

"I will send you our itinerary within the hour," Mrs. Scholz said, crisply, still stroking her husband's head, while staring at Adele. Those cold, calculating eyes didn't blink. "Every transaction, every meal, and everyone we spoke to in Amsterdam. There was no time for brothels. No time for whores. I can see what you're thinking. My husband didn't kill anyone. Neither did I. I wouldn't expect you to take our word for it, though. I'll give you our itinerary, financial statements. And if you are saying this prostitute of his was killed in the last two days, then you've clearly made a mistake."

"What mistake?" Adele said, feeling a sense of dread.

"We didn't get back from Amsterdam until this morning."

"Your flight said it came in yesterday," John interrupted, "at dawn."

Mrs. Scholz shook her head. "Check again. The plane was delayed. Unless you think we flew some other way, and had two stooges take our seats, we couldn't have been here. This whore wasn't killed this morning, was she?"

Adele let out a faint sigh. She shook her head. Besides, the person they had seen on the camera wasn't a woman. Mr. Scholz had an alibi. His own wife was providing it. Still, there was always the offchance they were being fooled.

"Financial statements and itinerary and a copy of those tickets," Adele said crisply. "And you will both need to come down to the station to give a statement. Bring your lawyer or not, you still have to come."

"Are you arresting us?"

Adele paused, inhaling shakily. She played the video footage in her mind. A man, wearing a hat, who had clearly scoped out the brothel. Not someone who had rapidly squeezed in a quick fling between a heavy schedule. No. It couldn't be.

"You're not under arrest. But don't leave the country. Not until they've taken a statement. And send me those details."

Adele hated to do it, but she turned her back on the Scholzs. She inhaled shakily, closing her eyes for a brief moment. She could still picture the terror in Gloria's expression, could still sense the fear.

But what was the point in pushing this further?

It seemed clear enough. Mr. Scholz had a far hardier wife than he must have first assumed. Whether he lost his job or marriage, none of it mattered. He wasn't the killer. Either he was acting, or he really had loved Monique. Which meant, horribly, they were back to square one.

Adele hissed through her teeth, raised her head, and marched stiffly back through those double doors, without giving the satisfaction of a glance back towards the two tycoons.

***

Adele stood outside the rotating glass door of the large office complex. She peered through the glass where John was jotting down information from the receptionist. Her father was pushing through the door, frowning as he approached. The evening air wafted across her skin in cool gusts. The parking lot now sat empty.

Faint moonlight reflected off the glass building. It seemed beautiful in a way. And yet Adele preferred trees.

She shivered, jamming her hands into her pockets, glancing towards where John was accepting printed files from the receptionist.

She just couldn't bear to do it herself. Another dead end. Another miss. She felt like she had lost her edge.

And she knew why.

Her father stepped out onto the cold sidewalk, moving towards her. There was something so comforting and so alarming at the same time about his familiar gait. More like lumbering, or a waddle. It would've been silly on anyone else. But she knew his stiff leg was from an injury on the job. Her father loved his job. He'd always loved his career. As a Sergeant, he hadn't made it far, but he had taken the job seriously. What he didn't have in talent or people skills he had made up for in being a relentless pitbull. He never let anything go. The one thing he loved most was the law.

This was a man who lived by the rules.

She stared as her father approached.

His expression softened. It seemed to pain him to do so as if he wasn't quite sure what muscles to use.

But when he drew nearer, his eyes were gentle. He reached out, hand as stiff as a plank of wood and patted her on the shoulder then the head, then seemed to realize this wasn't right and returned to the shoulder again. "You did good," he said simply. "I'm glad I came."

"No traffickers to protect me from this time." Adele added a hollow chuckle. But the humor didn't land. Not that it was really a joke, more of an observation.

"Can't catch them all on the first try. Either way, maybe you'll find something in the financials."

Adele sighed, shaking her head. "I don't think it's him. I think I just missed it."

Her father shrugged. "Well, at least you're willing to admit when you're wrong. It's a good skill to have. Not everyone does." He smoothed his mustache and glanced off into the darkening night.

Adele wanted John to return. Wanted him to return *right now*. She could feel something rising in her. Something she didn't want to say. And yet what excuse was there now? He was being kind. The relationship was better than it had ever been. And she just couldn't face a case like this with a pendulum dangling over her head. She knew why she was distracted. She knew why she was missing things. Guilt. She hadn't told him yet. She needed to tell him. She knew that now.

And yet, she loathed the thought. One thing he loved more than everything, including his own daughter, was the law. This was a man of justice. A hard, taxing man. A God-fearing man. A man of the Proverbs, as he liked to call himself. A whole lot of law, very little mercy.

It had made her strong, growing up in his house. And yet she dreaded telling him. She had broken the law.

But his eyes were gentle. His posture uncomfortable, but close to her. The pat on the head and shoulder hadn't quite been a hug, but it had been close enough. He was showing affection. He had even come with them to protect her. Her father was doing his best. So how could she dare not to do the same?

Besides, a small voice said in her head, *you can't keep distracting yourself. You have to come clean. Remove the mental block. Tell him.*

She glanced past her father, hoping John would push through the rotating door that very moment. But he was still by the reception desk, waiting as the woman printed another slew of papers. She had time, space.

"Dad," she said quickly. Even this word stung her lips.

He grunted.

"I think I need to tell you something. I *want* to tell you something. But I'm not sure you're going to like it."

Her father frowned at her. "You're pregnant." It wasn't a question.

He stated it as if he knew, like some harlequin detective revealing a key bit of evidence.

She blinked. "What?"

"That gorilla has impregnated you. I knew it. Adele, you shouldn't be sleeping with a man you're not married to."

She massaged her forehead. If she could've picked a way to start this conversation, she wasn't sure this would have made it in the top one hundred list. "Dad, listen, I'm not pregnant. This isn't about John."

"That's his name. John. So hard to remember."

Adele rolled her eyes. "Yeah, John. Super hard. Look, Dad, forget about him."

"I try to every day, my dear."

"I'm serious. It's about mom's killer."

They both went quiet as an employee pushed through the glass doors. Adele stared at the man, willing for him to walk faster along the sidewalk. He seemed to sense her disapproval and picked up his pace, swinging his briefcase and hastening towards a parked BMW. A second later, the vehicle's headlight's blinked on, and he moved out of the parking lot.

"Dad," she tried again, "I need to tell you about that night."

"Adele, I'm sure it was hard. But there are psychologists for this. I really don't think you want me to—"

"This isn't about my feelings, Dad. I'm not having PTSD. Well, at least, not really."

"I see. Well... I mean, you did a good job, Adele. You did what I could never do. You caught Elise's killer." He was rattling words off now, as if trying to figure which key fit in a padlock.

There was no good way to say it. Maybe she ought to just blurt it out. But wouldn't that be worse?

She resisted the urge to scream or bite her tongue. She let out a faint sigh. "Dad," she said. "I killed him on purpose."

There it was. She'd said it. A prickle spread along her cheeks. Was it really the mental blockade she thought it was? She didn't feel any different. She didn't feel some weight of guilt lift from her shoulders. All she felt was uncomfortable. And concerned.

Her father blinked. "Good. You didn't miss. You don't generally shoot people accidentally."

"No, Dad, I mean I *killed him on purpose*. I didn't have to." She could feel her stomach churning. He was really going to make her spell it out. It felt like pulling teeth.

"What do you mean?" he said, his voice emotionless.

"I mean, he was drowning. Unarmed. I'd already shot him. And I stood there and watched him die." Now that she was saying it, Adele felt the words coming rapidly. It didn't feel like she was confessing, though. She'd been expecting guilt. But now, in that moment, she felt only defiance. But defiance against what? Her father's expectations? His passionate love of the law?

She didn't even realize what she was saying as she continued, "And I don't regret it. I'd do it again. I'm sad I broke the law. But I'm glad I killed him. I'm glad I didn't help him. He drowned, Dad. I could see the bubbles in the water. I could see him struggling. But I had shot him, so he couldn't get up. His hand was groping at the dirt. Almost as if he was begging for help. But I just stood there. I watched him die. I don't feel bad about it." She said this with a loud gasp. It was relieving to finally say it. Of course, it wasn't completely true. She had doubts. Guilt. She'd shared that with John. There was something about compassion that allowed a person, a soul, to speak the truest level of honesty. There was something about the cold, hard legalism that only allowed for defiance. It was a strange thing to consider standing there, facing her father.

He was watching her, without saying a word. He just studied her face. He didn't frown. Didn't recoil. He just stared.

There was always something her father had loved more than his daughter. He called it doing what was right. He called it justice.

And now, she let out a faint, shaking sigh. A breath she had been holding as she spoke. He didn't get angry. He didn't shout. He didn't scream.

Adele didn't feel much better. She didn't feel much different at all. She just stared at her father. And then he turned. Still without a word and he began to walk away. That funny, stiff legged walk, from his old work injury. Hurt in the line of duty. He marched away from her, up the sidewalk.

"Dad," she protested, "how are you gonna get home?"

He didn't look back. He didn't say a word. He just jammed his hands into his pockets and moved away from her. He hunched a bit, and somehow, horribly, he seemed smaller than before. Deflated. Less.

And Adele had done it.

She stared as her father turned up the corner, disappearing around the edge of the office building.

The chill of the night descended on her. She felt a faint shiver.

And then even the sound of her father's footsteps disappeared.

"There's no way," she murmured to herself, "that could have possibly," she continued, feeling a deep pit in her stomach, "gone worse."

And even still, with her father marching away, Adele still had a case to solve. They were back to square one. At a dead end. Adele released a small sigh, turning to move towards her parked car and wait for John.

CHAPTER TWENTY FIVE

This club was different than the others. And it made sense she would be here of all places. He smiled to himself, peering up at the dark windows. The name of the club wasn't written anywhere. It was a word-of-mouth establishment, for the ultra-wealthy. He had been forced to be creative with some of his personal details on the phone when scheduling his appointment. But it was her. He knew it beyond a shadow of a doubt.

He was close. How many years had it been? How long? He had suffered without her. He had made a mistake. His hand bunched in his pocket, around the silk scarf. The only item she had left behind. Sometimes, if he took a moment, he could still smell her on it. What was life without love anyway?

A painful lesson, but one he had been forced to learn. In some ways, one he had taught himself.

Ahead, along the side of the building was a large, steel door. No visible handholds. No bouncers. No guests. It looked almost like a blank wall. Above, the darkened windows looked like they were shielding some warehouse.

But he knew better. This was the address they had given him.

She was here. The woman who broke his heart.

He waited on the sidewalk, hands in his pockets, blinking behind his spectacles; they had told him he might have to wait a bit. For first timers, there were a lot of background checks. The exorbitant fees of a place like this might have made him laugh in another life. But when they had asked for half up front, he had been happy to empty his account. He'd already spent thousands traveling, searching, hiring private investigators. From brothel to brothel, club to club. He had searched, calling, scrutinizing online photos. Always trying to find her. The search had started a few months ago. When he had seen a picture from Amsterdam. A beautiful, tall, blonde woman in a window; a tourist photo. But he thought he'd recognized her. He could even now remember how his heart skipped a beat. How could he forget a woman like that? The one that got away.

He smirked, standing on the sidewalk outside that big blank metal door. There was a buzzing sound. The door suddenly slid open. A man tucking his shirt in was whistling and gave a quick nod as he hurried up the sidewalk, moving in the other direction. The man's shoes alone were as expensive as most people's cars.

The lover watched him leave, curious. The john finished tucking his clothing in, then disappeared into a gated parking lot.

The door was still somewhat open; the lover glanced back, peering into the large space.

A flash of golden hair. A large man blocking the view, a clipboard in hand. A long leg, beyond the guard. The faint, crystalline laugh of a woman. A laugh he knew so well. His heart pounded. His throat constricted. "Madeline!" he called out, his voice hoarse.

But the door slid shut with another buzz.

His pocket vibrated, and with a shaking hand he removed his phone. A text from the club.

Five minutes longer.

He could wait another five minutes.

He glanced back in the direction of the gated parking lot. An expensive sports car, which he didn't recognize, was pulling out of the lot, onto the street. The lover wondered if that man in the car had just spent time with Madeline. He felt white-hot rage. But he swallowed it. That was what had gotten him in trouble last time, wasn't it? If he wanted her, he had to learn to share. He'd been naïve back in Belgium. Back where he had first fallen in love. He hadn't minded giving her money and buying her nice things. He'd been courting her. He hadn't known about the others. He hadn't known what she did for a living. Not until he *told* her.

"I love you," he'd murmured. He had even bought her a ring. And she had laughed at him: not a derisive laugh, but a piteous one. He'd been a small, sad man in her eyes. Of course, she had said all the right things. She'd pretended to be kind. But he had seen the derision in her eyes. And he had loathed it.

He reached up, adjusting his glasses, wiping a tear forming in the corner of one eye. A tear from sadness, but also anger and shame. He never should've reported her for breaking regulations. She'd vanished without a trace. And she had taken his heart with her.

He had failed in his attempt to find her. Nowhere in Belgium. None of the clubs. Nowhere he looked. It had been a divine blessing that he had seen that tourist photo from Amsterdam. Dumb luck. He'd searched the wrong entry online. He had been looking for local brothels. But it had been corrected to *famous* brothels. And so he'd found the woman in the glass.

His hands shook as he remembered how that had ended. She'd been a pretender. Not Madeline. A poser. And so he'd done what needed to be done. Madeline's scarf had been tight in his hands. The fake woman had died. She'd deserved it. He'd been careful after that. Double checking cameras, looking for proper ways in without being spotted. It all felt so exciting. Like a spy in the movies. And here he was now, looking for his long-lost love.

He smiled to himself, and reached into his pocket, pulling out the small, crumpled piece of paper.

He cleared his throat, his palm feeling sweaty all of a sudden. He glanced at the paper, reading the lines again. Just a small speech. Was the love poem too much?

Perhaps. Perhaps it was best that he saved the poem for later.

He shifted, glancing at his phone again. Only a few minutes remaining.

He felt uncomfortable, standing on the sidewalk exposed like this. But he'd come so far. He'd spent so much. He wouldn't go home without her. He could still picture the way she smiled. The way she had held him. A beautiful woman. A stunning woman. He could wait just a little bit longer. It couldn't possibly hurt to wait.

***

The adrenaline junkie had made his choice. There were a few ways he could do this. He scanned the building, smirking to himself.

First the girlfriend.

He could go through the window, or the apartment door. It didn't really matter. He hadn't brought a weapon with him. This one he would do up close and personal. Besides, with his training, nearly everything could be turned into a weapon. She would die at the hands of her own cutlery. Maybe a spoon. He giggled at the thought but caught the expression. Too much emotion and the scars along his face throbbed.

He clenched his teeth, and moved up the sidewalk, scanning the tall apartment building.

He could wait for someone to buzz in and follow after. That would be simple enough. He would have to check the door for any cameras. Law enforcement officers could often be paranoid.

Agent Renee's own home was out of the question.

"Agent," he murmured beneath his breath. He snorted in derision.

What a silly title for the Captain. And yet, everything about this game was deadly serious.

A game John had started ten years ago.

And a game *he* was going to finish.

A queen's gambit.

Except instead of sacrificing anything he had, he was going to sacrifice John's queen.

He nodded. Would he torture her? Do other things? Maybe just kill her?

He moved towards the apartment door, watching as a woman made her way down the stairs. The door buzzed, and he ducked his head, smiling politely, then slipped through.

The woman didn't even glance at him.

Yes. He would let the queen choose how she went. The two of them would play a little game as well.

The same sort of game John had played.

If she screamed or made a noise, he would hurt her horribly. If she stayed quiet, he would make it painless.

That was fair, wasn't it?

Behind him, through the closing door, he heard a sudden *bang!* A car? A gunshot. He tensed, his heart pounding. His vision swam, and all-too-real memories swirled back. He could feel the coarse, hot sand beneath his cheek. Could hear Captain Renee barking orders.

"To safety! Behind the dunes—go! Go!"

Renee had taken out five of the enemy on his own, holding up the rear, keeping his men safe. More gunshots sparked the hill-line. Rocket propelled grenades peppered their escape route. He could still smell the burning fuel of the downed helicopter. Could still feel the sweat along his cheeks, his eyes wide, his mouth hanging open.

Something had just come over him. A panic—a deep, bone-chilling terror. He'd screamed as if from a nightmare, tried to rip free from Renee.

And that's when he'd felt it.

War hero, John Renee had struck him. Hard. No warning whatsoever—at least, none he could remember. Then again, it had all been so chaotic. So much violence, so many explosions. Nothing he could do but go limp. His body had collapsed. The sounds had faded.

The adrenaline junkie blinked, biting his lip and tasting copper. It took him a second to realize his lower lip was bleeding. Shit. Sometimes the PTSD just triggered.

He scowled to himself. Renee had knocked him unconscious then thrown him to the wolves. Had left him for those little sand-dwelling torturers to rip him to shreds.

He wasn't sure what had been more painful. The torture or the following surgeries trying to put him back together. He let out a shaky little exhale, forcing himself to focus on the task at hand.

He could reminisce later.

He moved up the stairs slowly, eyes attentive, searching for neighbors or door cameras or anything else that needed to be avoided. He had always been cautious. It was one of his best skills.

He smirked as he moved up the floor.

It had been stunningly easy to find Agent Adele Sharp's address. Just a little backdoor, using credentials he'd once had that had never been revoked.

Bureaucrats were paid far too much.

There, her door. No camera. He would have to check the hinges in the frame.

He glanced up and down the hall, emitting a soft little giggle. Maybe he would even sleep on her bed. She was out of town. He knew that much. On a case with John of all things.

It almost made the whole situation delectable.

He didn't make a sound as he worked. Ducking low, pulling his pick and tension wrench from his pocket. He'd once worked on machines with far greater stakes for a missed turn of the wrist, or an un-loosened screw. One of these old building locks in Paris was no problem.

The door *clicked*. He smiled like a crocodile.

If she screamed, she would experience pain like she had never imagined. Not ten years of it like he had. He didn't have the luxury of that. If he could, with John, he might take his time. He had even fantasized about going away to a small little cabin he had rented in the mountains. Taking John with him. Pulling him apart a piece at a time over the course of years. That would be an easy life.

He paused, pocketing his toolset.

He allowed himself a little fantasy of the future.

Fishing, hunting, spelunking, exploring the woods, and coming home after a long day for a lovely dinner of freshly caught trout and lemon wedges. And then a quick trip to the woodshed where he would peel Renee like a grape.

A simple life. A fulfilling life.

He could see himself doing that for a good while.

Ten years? As long as he had suffered?

Hard to tell. But it was worth a try. A boy could dream.

He chuckled, silently, and pushed into the apartment.

But first things first. Agent Adele Sharp.

He glanced around the apartment. A couple dishes in the sink. But otherwise immaculate. He would live here for a day or two, depending on how long it took for them to get back.

What if John returned with her?

He wrinkled his nose. He would have to be careful, quiet. But if that happened, it could be fun in a different way. He could make John watch.

Yes. It was all going perfectly to plan.

He turned, beginning to close the door behind him. But then he glanced down and spotted something next to the hinges.

His eyes narrowed. "Hello there," he murmured. He dropped slowly to a knee, staring.

Clever. She was clever.

He'd have to be careful.

He reached for the ripped piece of tape.

But she wasn't clever enough.

CHAPTER TWENTY SIX

Adele paced up and down the hall outside the interrogation room back at the precinct. The Dortmund police force had accommodated her request.

But now, as she paced, Adele wasn't sure what to do next.

She could feel John watching her, standing in the lounge, his eyes hooded, his large arms crossed.

Agent Renee hadn't said anything on the drive back from Scholz industries. A bust. The itineraries, the tickets, the financials all checked out. John had asked about her father, but Adele had ignored this as well. She'd been glad they taken separate cars as she had needed the drive back to the precinct to think.

And now, as she tried to summon her resolve, her mind was whirring.

She glanced towards the steel door, considering her options. She was right. There was only one source of information that could help her here.

But what was the right question?

She paused, exhaling slowly at the metal door. Her hands were sweaty, prickling. She heard voices down the long hall as more police moved through the station.

"Is his lawyer still in there?" John called out.

Adele gave a quick, curt shake of her head. "Not right now. He'll be back in a few hours. Technically, were not supposed to talk to him."

She looked at John and shrugged.

He shrugged back.

She said, "Which is why I'm not going to ask him anything incriminating. Hell, maybe we can even cut a deal."

John didn't say anything, still watching her, like a spectator at the zoo.

Adele sighed faintly and ran back through the information. She couldn't sulk. Her father's actions hurt. He had just walked away. But she couldn't let it get to her. Another woman would die if she didn't figure this out.

So where was the mistake? She'd confessed to her dad. That had been the blockage. So what had she missed?

The killer clearly had a type. Belgian. Blonde. Beautiful. Tall. Just like Adele. That's what the executive had said. She looked like the victims.

Which was why they were back here. Maybe that was the mistake. It wasn't about looking *like*.

Maybe the killer wasn't interested in a type. But a person.

It was the only thing left. The last straw she had to grasp. The killer was looking for someone specific. An individual. Just like that brother trying to drag his sister from the brothel. The killer was hunting someone. And when he didn't find them, his rage took over. He strangled them.

It fit. It had to fit.

Adele slammed her hand into her palm. A loud smack.

So what was the question?

Adele suddenly reached out, grabbing the handle and swinging open the door. She stomped into the interrogation room, her eyes landing on the olive-skinned human smuggler sitting behind the table. He had that same easy look about him. His hands were folded in his lap, the handcuffs nearly invisible by the way his fingers splayed across the knuckles. He watched her, unblinking. As she came to a halt in front of the table, he flashed a smile.

"I have a question," Adele said.

"You're not supposed to be here without my lawyer."

"This isn't about your case. I need your help."

He stared at her. "And what will I get in return?"

Adele wanted to slam her hand against the table. They didn't have time for games. But she kept her cool. "I'll put in a good word. I'll ask them to reduce your sentence."

He stared at her. "Immunity."

"That's not possible."

"Immunity or my lips are sealed."

Adele's hand bunched into a fist at her side. She pretended she was scratching her leg, uncurling her fingers again. The business with her father, with the mistake at the giant office building, with all of it was fraying her at the seams. She didn't need this smartass to pile on.

"Just answer my question," she barreled on. "You said you remembered all the women you smuggled. Is that right?"

"I also said unless I get immunity I'm not going to talk."

Adele let out a long puff of air. She glared, her mind spinning. She didn't have the jurisdiction to guarantee something like that. She could lie, perhaps. But that grated against her character. So many things could be justified by saying a life was on the line. But the things it justified were sacred to her. Honesty, fairness.

No, she wouldn't lie. But he was playing his cards with a smug look on his face. In this situation, she didn't mind applying a little leverage.

"I still have that business card of yours," she said. "Imagine what's going to happen to your reputation if I let it be known to all the girls at that club that you were arrested. Not only that, two of the women you were going to traffic were arrested as well. I'll tell everyone. I don't care. I don't have plans this weekend. I'll get some of the prostitutes at the club to tell their friends. I'll pay them myself to spread the information." She raised a crook of her hand as if blocking out letters on a billboard. In an announcer's voice she declared, "Don't trust Baris or his business. He'll get you killed or arrested."

As she spoke, his smile faded.

Adele didn't feel an ounce of regret as she lowered her hand. This man had made money off human desperation. All he cared about was his business.

Baris glared at her over his clasped fingers. "You're not playing fair."

"I'm not playing at all. This isn't a game. Same deal I said. I'll keep my word. I'll put in a request on your behalf. Sentence leniency. That's it. I can't do immunity"

He let out a long sigh. He closed his eyes briefly, and his head swayed as if hearing some faint, distant music. Then, his eyes snapped open. "What do you want to know?"

Adele felt a surge of excitement. Her hands clasped the back of the metal chair on the other side of the table. The door was shut behind her. The two of them were alone in the interrogation room. She couldn't bring herself to sit. She was too on edge. So standing, staring down at him, she said, "You remember the girls you smuggled. That's what you said."

"I did. I do."

"Blonde," Adele said, "Belgian, pretty. Tall."

He stared at her. "What about it?"

"I need you to think of all the women you've worked with who fit that description. *All* of them."

He frowned, his expression flickering. "You said this wasn't about me."

"It's not. I'm trying to narrow down my potential targets. Please."

"Well, you already know about Monique."

"Yes, and the woman in Amsterdam. I'm talking others. People who aren't dead. People who we haven't thought of. *Please.*"

The trafficker let out a little grunt of pleasure. As if it pleased him to have something Adele needed. He took his time about it, leaning back in his chair, closing his eyes and tilting his head.

"Well?" Adele demanded.

He opened one eye, looking at her like a lazy cat. "This isn't easy. Give me a second, I'm remembering." He closed his eyes again. Adele bit her lip, but this time kept her silence.

The human trafficker sat quietly, his eyes twitching, as if his eyeballs were moving behind his otherwise calm demeanor. His head tilted to the side, he paused briefly, but kept his eyes closed.

Then, faintly, he said, "Two. Two other women. And mind you, that's from nearly half a decade of business."

Adele stared. He still kept his eyes closed. "I don't remember their last names. It's been a while. But there was one woman named Devana. And another one named Natalie."

"They were both Belgian?"

He nodded once. He still kept his eyes shut. The effect was quite eerie. "Both blonde, both beautiful. Both tall. And both Belgian."

"I need their last names."

He opened his eyes now, though, shrugging. "I'm sorry, but I can't remember. That's all I have."

Adele hesitated, meeting his gaze. He seemed to be telling the truth. Without a last name, it would make things harder... but when had they ever come easy? She reached a decision and was already turning, hastening back towards the door.

"Hang on!" he called after her. "What about me?"

"I'll put a good word in!" she called back. "Thank you!"

She shoved through the door, rushing back out into the hall where John was still waiting, frowning towards the interrogation room.

When she emerged again, he perked up, staring. "Everything okay?"

"We need access to BKA's database," Adele said quickly. "We'll have to go through Interpol. Whatever channel is fastest. But we need the names of all the legally registered prostitutes in Germany."

"Did he give you something?"

Adele was nodding hurriedly, racing towards the break room where John's briefcase rested on the table. She gestured at it frantically. "Boot it up. Come on!"

While Agent Renee unzipped the bag to pull out his laptop, Adele's foot tapped a tattoo into the floor. "Two names," she said. "Only two.

But he didn't have last names."

John frowned, booting up the computer. "What names?"

"Devana and Natalie," Adele said quickly. "It might not be enough based on name, but if they have pictures of the registered prostitutes, we could narrow it down."

John entered his login information. The air was tense. They both went quiet as John continued with two-factor authentication to access the DGSI database they used to make requests with Interpol.

"What if they're not registered?" John said, voicing the question pinballing in Adele's mind.

"We'll cross that bridge when we get to it," she snapped. "We're probably already out of time, John. The killer is gonna keep going until we stop him. This is the only option."

Renee sighed but nodded. He entered something on the keyboard, frowned, waited a few moments, then said, "Good. We're in. Pre-cleared."

Adele leaned over John's shoulder. "This is it? All the files from Germany?"

John shook his head. "Most recent ones from the BKA. We're pre-approved. But not further back than five years."

"Five years is fine," Adele said hurriedly. "Come on John. Hurry."

Her partner entered the first name. Devana. Nearly instantly, a list of names appeared on the screen throughout Germany.

"More than seventy," John said with a low whistle. "That's a lot."

"Refine by age," Adele said. "20s and 30s."

John nodded entering the new parameters.

"Forty names," he said.

"Refine by height," Adele countered. "Driver's licenses should log it."

John frowned, nodding again.

"Twenty names," he said.

Adele could feel her heart pounding. "Can we refine by hair color?"

"Might have it dyed."

Adele cursed, but then said, "They have pictures. They have to have pictures for the licenses. Open them."

Meticulously, one by one, John opened new browser tabs with photographs of the remaining twenty women named Devana.

"Not her," Adele said quickly. She shook her head. Again and again, she said, "No. Nope. Too small. Brown hair. Not pretty enough."

They cycled through the list. They reached the last name. Devana Johnson.

John clicked on the name. The woman looked like she was in her forties, even though the license said she was thirty.

Adele growled. "It's none of them. Dammit."

John sighed. "Maybe Devana isn't registered."

"Again. Let's go through the photos again."

They did, slower this time. But the women didn't look anything like the previous victims. Adele could feel her heart plummet.

"What was that other name?" John said, trying to keep them on track.

Adele's stomach twisted, but she said, "Natalie."

John entered the new name. He refined the parameters once more. And again, Adele could feel her pulse racing out of control. And again, they narrowed down to a list of names. Only ten this time.

One by one, they opened the photographs and cycled through. "This one doesn't have a photo," John said with a frown.

Adele tapped the screen. "Deceased," she said. She felt a jolt of sadness but didn't have the time to linger on compassion. "Not her. Move on."

John cycled through the last few photos.

Simultaneously, they both perked up. "Her," John and Adele said at the same time.

They stared at the photo on the screen. A beautiful, blonde woman. She had fresh features. According to her license, she was five-foot-nine

"She looks just like that woman in Amsterdam," Adele said hurriedly.

John was nodding, already copying the information.

"I'm texting it to us," he said. "But what about Devana? What if she's the actual target?"

Adele fidgeted uncomfortably. John messaged the details where Natalie worked to Adele's phone. She paused, fingers hovering over her pocket. Then, with a snarl of frustration, she said, "You stay here. Keep researching. Start contacting any criminal databases to see if someone fitting Devana's description was caught for any illegal prostitution. I don't know, whatever you need John. Pull out all the stops. You need to find this woman."

"That's a needle in a haystack."

"You need to find her. Natalie looks like the woman from Amsterdam. But that was the whole point. They all did. It could still be Devana."

John leaned back in his chair, scowling up at her. "And what are you going to do?"

"What do you think," Adele said, turning on her foot, and breaking into a jog. John tried to call after her, but Adele didn't hesitate. She had to reach Natalie. The woman was the spitting image of the other victims. The killer was already on the move—he would kill again. They always did.

John would have to find their missing Cinderella. One of these women, Adele was certain, would be the next victim. The same trafficker had dealt with two of the victims from Belgium. Either she had missed it again, or she was right on target.

She ignored the strange glances from other police officers as she jogged through the lobby, through the sliding, glass doors, and hastened down the steps towards her parked car. She ripped her phone from her pocket, double checking the address where Natalie still worked. A club about twenty miles away.

Nearly a thirty-minute drive in German traffic. She could only hope Natalie still had thirty minutes.

CHAPTER TWENTY SEVEN

Adele screeched into the parking space. It struck her as strange that a brothel would have handicap spot. "Civilization," she muttered beneath her breath, throwing open the door and slamming it. She locked the vehicle behind her as she hastened towards the inconspicuous entrance.

The door was half open, and a figure was emerging.

The person in question was an older man, with a satisfied expression. One look at Adele, in her suit, coming from the tinted windowed car, and he frowned, ducking his head and picking up the pace.

She heard him mutter, "Cop."

She didn't care, she rushed towards the open door. As she tried to slip through, though, a big, meaty hand shoved out to push her back.

"Stop," the voice said.

"Police," Adele snapped. She flashed her identification, her jacket opening to reveal her side arm.

The big guy in the door, instead of looking concerned, looked irritated. "Can't you read?" said the gorilla.

He had no neck. One of his ears was missing. And he looked like his father had probably been a football player and his mother a cement mixer.

The man was nearly as wide as Adele's car.

He stood in the gap of the sliding door, glaring at her. He pointed towards her gun. "No weapons."

He indicated a sign next to him, with a list of banned contraband.

Adele hissed, "I'm with Interpol. Get out of my way."

The guy didn't budge an inch. "You can come in. The gun stays outside."

She just stared at him, stunned. "I don't have time for this."

He didn't move. Adele had to reach a quick decision. She might have been able to arrest him and get him out of her way. But the altercation would take too long.

With a hiss, she spun on her heel, sprinted back towards her car in a flurry of footsteps, unlocked the vehicle, ripped her holster off her hip and tossed it into the car. She shut the door, locked it again, and turned to face the guard. She opened her jacket to show her empty hip. "Happy?"

He stepped aside, bored. "Customer or provider?"

Adele jostled past him, hastening into the brothel. "Neither," she snapped.

She looked frantically around. The atmosphere inside the untoward establishment was cozy. A crackling fire and hearth. Club sandwiches on silver trays. Drinks in chalices rather than cups. Women in long dresses, with beautiful earrings escorted scruffier looking men through the place. Some of them moved upstairs towards rooms. Others laughed and guided the men out behind the building toward a steaming swimming pool.

Adele's gaze bounced around the space. It was far more attractive on the inside than the outside.

She wasn't sure what to make of this.

She took a moment to realize she was standing alone, unarmed. But it was too late to turn back. Back-up was on its way. She'd already placed a call in her breakneck race to the club. But they were minutes out. She wasn't sure she had minutes.

She reached out, snagging the arm of one of the waitresses. The woman had a low-cut top, a tantalizing smile, and swishing diamond earrings. "May I help you?" the woman said. She began to extend a tray with small, fruit beverages.

But Adele ignored the tray. "Natalie, where is she?"

The waitress still smiled but looked confused. "Excuse me?"

"She's tall, blonde, pretty. Belgian. *Natalie*."

The waitress's eyes widened. "Um, maybe you should speak with the manager."

Adele's grip tightened on the woman's wrist. Not hard enough to hurt, but firm enough to make it clear she wasn't going to let go without a struggle. "Please," Adele said, "where is she?"

The waitress's eyes darted up the stairs. "With a client," she said, with a whisper. "If you want an appointment you have to speak to the manager. Now please, the gentleman over there wants a drink."

Adele released her grip, hastening towards the stairs and taking them two at a time.

She needed her weapon. But she couldn't go back to get it. The bouncer would cause more trouble.

She growled beneath her breath. Part of her hoped, desperately, that John was able to track down the second woman. If she was wrong about this. If she had taken a shot and missed, they would need that second name. That second location.

But now, she felt a slow, daunting sense of unease.

She could feel, deep in her bones, that she was getting closer. She hastened down the hall, kicking open a door.

A scream, a shout.

"Sorry," Adele hissed, wincing. Wrong skin color. Wrong hair color. Wrong gender.

She moved on to another door and pushed this one open.

No one was inside. She could hear the shower water running followed by giggling. Playful laughter.

Adele cursed, moving on to the next door. She pushed this one open too.

From behind her, she could hear angry voices. It sounded like the thick bouncer. Stomping footsteps thundered up the stairs.

Her eyes landed on two figures on the bed.

A cozy, well lit room. Another fireplace, but this one electric.

Her gaze, though, was drawn to the two figures.

A man crouched over a blonde woman, his hands around her neck.

The woman was wheezing, the man gasping. His fingers tightened on the woman's throat. Her legs kicked.

Adele shouted, barreling into the room. She flung herself at the killer, knocking him off the bed. The two of them hit the ground. Adele's shoulder struck floorboards with a loud *crack!*

The man she'd tackled groaned, flopping onto a carpet in front of the fireplace. The woman, half naked, screamed, tugging the blankets up and around her.

Adele gasped, "Are you okay?" she said. "Are you all right?"

The woman on the bed was Natalie. The blonde hair, the beauty. She looked as if she hadn't aged a day since her license picture.

The only difference was the glare. She was scowling at Adele and slipped off the edge of the bed, moving towards where the man was still groaning. She patted him on the chest, rubbing her fingers through knotted chest hair. "I'm so sorry, dear. I don't know who this crazy bitch is."

Adele stared.

The woman glared at Adele again, still stroking the john's chest hair. "Idiot woman," she snapped. "What do you think you're doing?"

Adele gaped, blinking. "He was choking you!"

"And he paid handsomely to do it," she retorted. "You just cost me my rent."

Adele stared. The woman didn't seem harmed at all. She was

breathing regularly enough.

A slow, sinking realization of dread filled Adele. She glanced at the man on the ground. Too fat. He wasn't the man from the video feed. He was now trying and struggling to sit up. Too old. This wasn't the killer. She'd made a horrible mistake.

She heard a loud *thump* and looked back to see the bouncer in the door, glaring at her, a finger pointing.

Adele returned the angry look. "Touch me, and this time I *will* arrest you."

The bouncer yelled, "Get out!"

Adele glanced once more at the prostitute, making sure she was okay. All she received for her trouble was a rude hand gesture.

The prostitute went back to consoling the dazed man on the ground.

Adele pushed shakily to her feet, exhaling. "He'll be fine," she said. "The floorboards cracked, not him."

She rubbed at her shoulder, wincing, adjusting her sleeves if only to preserve some amount of dignity.

This wasn't their killer. This woman might not be the target at all.

What if the killer came back tonight, though?

Adele looked at the woman who was still glaring, and said, with as even a tone as she could manage, "I'll highly advise you: don't take anymore choking clients. Please."

"You crazy bitch."

"You're welcome," Adele muttered. She would have to place a police officer outside the club until the killer was caught, just in case he came for Natalie later.

But that still left the question. Where was Devana? Was John any closer to finding the second potential victim?

She moved towards the door. The bouncer reached out as if to grab her wrist, but Adele said, "If you want to keep your testicles, keep your fingers to yourself."

The bouncer hesitated, looked at her, and then withdrew his hand.

"Get out, copper," he snapped. "No warrant, no more entry! Leave!"

She massaged the bridge of her nose, wincing from her throbbing shoulder. She took a far different type of walk of shame than these halls were most accustomed to. But she picked up the pace towards the top of the stairs. She didn't look back. She didn't need to know three sets of eyes were glaring after her.

She took the stairs hurriedly, moving back towards the exit and pulled her phone from her pocket, breathing heavily. She placed a call, slipping out towards her car once more.

"John?" She said quickly, "he's not here. Not yet. I'll post someone outside the brothel, but we still need to find Devana."

John replied, quickly, "Found her."

"You did?"

"Petty theft arrest record. Yes. Busted for prostitution. But let off without any charges. Some type of deal."

"Not sure I want to know what type of deal gets you out of those types of charges," Adele muttered. She hurried towards the car now, slipping into the vehicle.

"I'm sending you the address; I'll meet you there."

Adele turned on the engine, and glanced at her phone, waiting for Agent Renee's text, her heart pounding fit to burst.

CHAPTER TWENTY EIGHT

It was finally the lover's turn.

He felt like a little schoolboy, waiting outside the principal's office. It had been years since he'd been this nervous.

He twisted back and forth, shifting uncomfortably in the hallway outside the closed bedroom door.

The usher had shown him to the room. The final comment of, "She might be another few minutes," had unsettled him, but again, he reminded himself that he needed to have an open mind for this to work. He couldn't allow jealousy to keep them apart. Not again. He missed her too much.

And yet every giggle and quiet grunt coming from the room beyond was like a dagger to his chest

He stood in the hallway, waiting his turn with his beloved.

He glanced at his phone. Not even a minute over the hour and the door suddenly cracked open.

He tried to glance into the room beyond, but only caught a glimpse of blonde hair, before a skinny, young fellow slipped out of the room. The man, though he was barely that, had fading hair, handsome features, and a mischievous grin. His cheeks reddened as he glanced towards the lover.

"Sorry," the man said quickly. "I didn't mean to take too much time. Anyway, she's all yours."

He patted the lover on the shoulder in a friendly gesture, and then hurried down the hall, towards the large, blank door at the end of the atrium.

The lover could feel his skin prickling where the man's fingers had tapped.

Revulsion filled him. He would have to wash his sleeve.

Part of him wanted to go after the young man and bludgeon him over the back of the head. As these fantasies played out in his mind, though, a voice called from the room beyond. "One moment!" A familiar, musical tone. "I'm just cleaning up."

He stared at the closed door. His heart pounded. He recognized that voice. How long had he waited to hear it again?

He could hear the sound of the shower running now. It was just like her clean-up for him—so considerate. So beautiful. Even her voice was mesmerizing like always.

He tentatively breached the door, and stepped into the bedroom, then closed the door behind him with a faint click.

And they were alone together again.

The en suite bathroom door was open, allowing a length of yellow light to spill into the bedroom. The bed was already made.

"Sheets are clean," a voice called from the shower. "We didn't use the bed!"

He gritted his teeth and moved towards the bathroom door.

"Almost done," she called. "Sorry, he was a new client. They sometimes take extra time to acclimate. Just a moment."

A faint steam was wafting from the open bathroom door.

He peered in, staring towards the shower. He could just about discern her outline through the foggy glass. Even without seeing her perfectly, he knew she was perfect.

Briefly, he thought his eyes were misting again. But then he realized the fog from the shower was clouding his glasses. He reached up hurriedly to wipe them clean.

And then he heard a faint gasp.

He stared, blinked, replaced his glasses, and realized she had emerged from the shower. Her hair was dripping wet. She had a towel hastily wrapped around her but had frozen in a cloud of mist, gaping.

He smiled, a shy, coy little grin. "Hello, Devana," he said softly. "I never thought you would actually use your real name."

She was shaking. Her hand trembled where it pressed against the glass door, trying to keep it open. "What are you doing here?" she said, her voice filled with emotion.

He beamed. She was clearly excited to see him. He could hear it in her voice. "I'm here for you. I'm so sorry how things ended. I never meant to chase you away." He gave a charming little flitter with his fingers. A sort of airy, dismissive gesture, as if tossing old, bad memories into the past.

"But it's going to be okay now," he said, with an assured nod. "We're together again."

She tugged her towel tighter around her frame. She'd always been modest. Especially for someone in her line of work.

He turned quickly, shaking his head. "I'm sorry. I didn't mean to come in here while you weren't dressed. Take your time. We have two hours to talk. I booked a double. I'm willing to try it your way now. I shouldn't have been jealous. I know that."

He could feel his own emotion welling up. His back was to her, and he faced the room again, giving her the privacy that she needed.

He heard the faint slap of bare feet against porcelain.

Her voice was still shaking, trembling with love. With affection.

"You should leave," she said as she got hurriedly dressed. He caught glimpses of rushed motion in the mirror.

He tensed. "What do you mean?"

"Please. I don't want any trouble. Please, but I'm going to call for security."

He hesitated, trying to understand what his lover meant. "Security?" he said, trying to piece together this mysterious puzzle. "You want someone else here with us? I suppose I understand. A test!" He said suddenly, realizing what she was up to. "Of course, a lover's test. Anything for you my dear. Just get dressed."

"I mean it, go away!"

There was something in her voice. He glanced back; his eyes widened. She was dressed now, but water stains spread across patches of her clothing. She was also holding a metal pole from the towel rack, clutching it in her hands.

"Well," he said, staring. "I mean, if that's what you want. I'm not sure, how comfortable that'll be."

She stared at him. He stared back.

She looked at the pole in her hand, and then her face twisted. "What? No. Get out of here!"

He turned his back on her again, shaking his head. "Now, now," he said softly, "dry off. I'm being patient. Can't you see I'm being patient? I've come a long way for you. This is my time. Two hours. I just want to talk."

A moment of silence, then a faint breath behind him, as if she were gathering her courage. Love always took courage.

He admired her for it. She'd always been someone to speak her mind.

And then a screech. A swishing sound, and a painful *thwack* across the back of his head.

He stumbled forward, wincing, hand moving up.

He twisted, staring, rubbing at his skull.

She was still holding the metal pole, trembling horribly.

"You hit me," he said, stunned.

"Get out of here!" she screamed.

"Be quiet," he retorted. "You'll ruin our time."

She tried to swing at him again. There was nothing sexy, nothing romantic about it. She was trying to hit him.

"You don't recognize me, do you?" he said, suddenly, feeling the weight of the moment. He let out a forced little chuckle, still rubbing his tender head. "We're going to laugh about this one day. With our kids. I'm so sorry. I thought you recognized me."

"I know who you are. I recognize you, Petar!"

He frowned. "But..." he trailed off.

If she knew who he was, why was she trying to hit him? She didn't look happy to see him; she looked angry, scared. What was happening?

He could feel his emotions in turmoil. He exhaled faintly, trying to piece it together. It didn't make sense. Why was she behaving so strangely?

"No, no, no," he murmured, his voice turning to a whine. "No, no," he said, louder.

Her face went pale, and she stared at him. She knew how he acted when he got like this. "Get out of here, please, I don't want trouble."

"I want you," he said. "We're in love. We've been in love!"

"You scare me, you creep. I don't want anything to do with you. I left the country to get away from you!"

"Don't say that," he said, his lips tightening. "Don't say that," he repeated with a snarl.

It was beginning to make sense. Someone had poisoned her against him. Someone had come here first. It was that skinny guy, wasn't it? He would find that guy too.

She inhaled faintly, preparing to scream.

He held a finger to his lips and quickly shook his head, holding out his hands and backing away. She didn't scream yet, as he moved back towards the door.

"Hang on," he said, "we can still make this work. This doesn't have to turn into something we'll both regret."

She stared at him, her eyes wide, her hand still gripping that metal rod. The rod she had hit him with.

She was poisoned. He'd come too late.

"No, no," he muttered beneath his breath, massaging his head. "No, no," he kept saying.

"LEAVE!"

"Please, just put that down, come over here. Give me a kiss. It's not too late. It doesn't have to be this way."

Something in the way he said it must've caught her attention. Her voice warbled. "What way?"

He turned back, grabbed the dresser, and with a couple of grunts, pulled it to block the door. He had a sad feeling now. He looked at her and said, "I didn't want it to end this way."

She let out a scream. But it didn't matter; it would take some time for the ushers to grab security. A place like this didn't seem to want big, tough looking men too visible for all their high-end clients. Part of the price tag came with a level of trust. The security guards were on a different floor. He had time. Besides, stranger sounds sometimes came from these rooms.

He reached into his pocket and pulled out an item, keeping it bunched in his hand.

"You left this behind," he said quietly. His sadness was turning to anger. Regret. He now knew what he had to do; he hated it though. Still, maybe there was still a chance. "Please," he said softly, "just come over here. Give me a hug; it's going to be okay."

She screamed again. He frowned, unclenching his fist. The long, silk scarf she'd left behind fluttered from his fingers, unfurling.

He gripped it in his other hand, tightening it.

"I didn't want to do this. Just so you know. I really didn't want to do this."

She screamed again.

He had no choice. She'd *left* him no choice.

So he rushed her.

CHAPTER TWENTY NINE

Adele's hands gripped the steering wheel as she tore through the city streets, careening through red lights and breezing past stop signs. A truck leaned on a horn as she veered around it, racing back towards the same club where Monique had been killed.

"Adele!" Agent Renee's voice barked over the Bluetooth speakers in the car, "What's that sound? Is someone honking at you?"

She gritted her teeth, growling as she spotted three cars stopped at a red light ahead. She muttered a little prayer, then veered off onto the shoulder, over a white line, and ripped through the red light, turning sharply to the right, and narrowly avoiding a collision with a taxi. More honking horns.

This damn car didn't have a siren. But it didn't matter, she was adamant about getting there in time.

Local police had been informed of the car she was driving. They wouldn't interfere with her en route.

"What's your ETA?" Adele barked, glancing at the GPS.

John hesitated, then replied, "Twenty-five minutes. You?"

"GPS says fifteen. So ten."

Another stop sign disappeared into the rearview mirror.

"Adele, don't kill yourself."

"You're the one who taught me how to drive like this, John!"

Renee muttered darkly; she heard the sound of a horn. But this time, it was coming over the speakers. She didn't doubt Agent Renee was taking similar maneuvers as he sped in the direction of the same club.

She glanced at the GPS. She had saved a minute.

"John," she said, her voice tight, mostly distracted, but also listening for her partner's response. "You're sure it's the same club?"

"She's not registered! DAMN IT, get out of the way! Umm, sorry. Yeah, I'm sure. I told you, she was caught soliciting at the club. Arrested. I spoke to the owner. She works in the same block. Different club. The same type of thing, though."

"The owner recognized her?"

Another blaring horn over the Bluetooth speakers. John descended into a slew of curses. After a moment, he cleared his throat, "Sorry, what was that?"

"The owner recognized her?"

"Hell yeah. Knew her immediately. Sounded a bit frustrated. I think the owner was trying to hire her, but this competitor poached her. Apparently, she's some sort of high-end prostitute. Only the richest sorts visit her."

"Cops on the way?"

John clicked his tongue. "A few. But you're gonna get there before they do."

Adele slammed her hand against the steering wheel.

She needed to go faster. Faster. She shoved her foot against the pedal, flooring it, speeding through the city.

The killer would be there. Unless he went after Natalie later tonight. But no, she'd already sent an officer to keep an eye on that particular potential victim. Devana was the only other woman who fit the description. And the killer hadn't struck in a while, which meant they were due for another murder.

"Be careful John," Adele said, gritting her teeth.

"Same to you."

She hung up. Her hands didn't leave the steering wheel, using the button beneath the windshield wipers.

Another screech of tires as she swerved around the truck. Faster, faster. No time to waste.

In a way, it didn't just feel like she was going towards something, but almost as if she were running *from* something.

This was a stray, unnerving, errant thought she wished she hadn't conjured.

What could she possibly be running from?

She even glanced in the rearview mirror. Besides a flash of headlights from an angry motorist, nothing was behind her. Things were clear. The painter was dead. Her mother avenged. John was on her side.

And yet, she knew eventually she might have to slow down.

Not in the car. Almost zombielike, she went through the motions of careening through traffic. How many times had she done something just like this?

No, but slowing down to grieve. Robert Henry. Her mother, even though that had been a decade ago. Her ex-fiancé.

Her own innocence.

She felt a flash of emotion. She didn't speculate what it was. She didn't allow it to be felt.

But her father would never see her the same.

She glanced at the speedometer. Couldn't this damn thing go any faster?

The GPS guided her towards the exclusive, high-end club on the same block as the FKK brothel.

And then, a faint chirping sound. *Arriving at destination on left.*

Adele resisted the urge to pump her fist. Her eyes were wide; she tore over a two-lane highway, jumping the curb.

She slowed as she reached the parking lot, carefully checking for pedestrians.

Ahead, she spotted a blank metal door with no visible sign above it. The windows were blacked out but there were cars in the parking lot. She frowned towards the metal door and glanced again at the GPS. This was where it was taking her.

The place didn't have much in the way of advertisement. Perhaps that was how the wealthier clubs did it.

She pushed out of the car, slamming the door, not even bothering to lock it as she sprinted up the steps. She pounded her fist against the metal. "Interpol!" she yelled. "Open!"

Almost immediately, after the first blow of her hand against metal, the door began to slide. The moment she screamed *Interpol*, though, the door redirected the other way, as if the person on the other side had changed their mind.

But Adele jammed her foot in the metal door, and growled, "Open the door, now!"

Slowly, the sliding metal frame opened. A sheepish face, above a suit and tie and a perfectly pressed outfit, stared out at her.

A man blinkeds beneath trimmed eyebrows. "Can I help you?" he said in exactly the sort of voice she might have imagined. Pretentious, droning, drawling.

"Get out of my way!"

It wasn't a request. She shoved past him.

The man took a few steps back, protesting weakly.

Adele glanced around the space. She'd never seen such opulence behind such an ordinary door before.

There was a private Koi pond in the center of a golden floor. Someone had converted the back half of an Aston Martin into a couch. Drinks were being served from behind crystal counters. Various clients moved throughout the space. Servers dressed in suits, thin, with handsome features and beady eyes moved among the guests. Gorgeous women draped over clients, laughing at jokes they didn't find funny, touching arms and faces they didn't find attractive.

The whole place had the stench of money.

Adele grabbed the steward by the shirt and looked him in the eyes. "Where is Devana?"

The man blinked. "Did you say you were with—"

"Interpol! *Where* is Devana? Tell me before I start arresting people."

He swallowed again. She hadn't even flashed an identification. But the man caved. He muttered something about not getting paid enough to go to jail and said, "Down the hall, the very last room. The client has paid for two hours, though."

Adele pushed past the steward, patting at his suit in a small gesture of appreciation.

She broke into a sprint, racing down the hall, towards the indicated door. Even the doorways struck her as ornamental. Golden filigree, pearlescent swooping designs etched in the metal. Paintings on the wall. Was that an original Van Gogh?

She focused, reaching the indicated door and slamming her hand against it. "Devana?" she called out.

She thought she heard a faint mutter.

She pounded harder. She tried the handle. Locked.

She definitely heard something now coming from inside the room. Grunting?

In a place like this that could mean a few things.

Still, better safe than sorry.

She gestured wildly down the hall towards the same steward who had allowed her through. "Help!" she shouted.

The man was in conference with another gentleman. The second fellow wore a charcoal suit and had silver temples. The sort of man who might be in charge. Adele caught the whispered word, "Interpol."

The man in the suit's face went the color of his clothing. He quickly backed away, muttering some instructions and then disappearing through a side door.

Interpol clearly opened doors around this place. At least one of the prostitutes wasn't licensed. But Adele wasn't here for that.

The steward hurried forward, a key card appearing in his hand.

His fingers were trembling so badly he dropped the card.

"Come on," Adele said urgently. She shouted at the door, "Devana, open up!"

But no one came to the door. The grunting sound stopped.

Adele's heart was trying to reach her throat.

"Come on, please, hurry up!"

With the same shaking hand, the steward inserted the key card into the slot. The light shifted from red to green and Adele yanked the door open.

At least, she tried to. But something was blocking it on the other side.

She cursed. "Is it chained?" she demanded of the steward.

He stared in horror and tried to card again. The light still flashed green. "There isn't any bolt or chain!"

"Help me," Adele demanded.

She was well past polite. She grunted, throwing herself at the door. The steward hesitated, but at a gesture from her, he joined in trying to push.

A crack appeared. Something was blocking the door on the other side.

Adele's finger scrambled through, and she felt the edge of a dresser. She pushed, groaning as she did. The steward helped her.

And then, she stumbled into the room. The piece of furniture on the other side crashed to the ground as she looked up.

Two figures on the bed. One of them crouched like a gargoyle over the other. A long strand of scarf in his hands, wrapped around a blonde woman's neck.

Adele thought back to the debacle with Natalie. But this was different. The woman wasn't moving. Her face was blue. Her eyes bulging. Saliva on her lips.

The man on top of her didn't look like much. A small man, with a mousy face and spectacles. He was sweating. But his muscles were taught in his forearms. He was crying. Tears fell from his eyes, and Adele realized what she had taken for saliva was actually a product of the man's weeping on the woman's face.

The steward behind her shouted. Adele charged. She flung herself at the killer.

Again, her already throbbing shoulder slammed into the strangler.

But he was quick. Quicker than he had first appeared. He jerked back, loosening his grip on the woman's neck. With the same motion, he dodged her momentum. Adele sprawled across the throttled woman. Did she feel a pulse? She didn't sound like she was breathing. Shit.

Adele tried to reach out and check the woman's neck with her fingers.

But the killer lunged in, grabbing at her forefinger and twisting it to break it.

Adele shouted in pain, bending backwards to avoid cracking her finger. With the same motion she shoved into the killer a second time.

He toppled now, hitting the pillows.

The steward was still shouting from the doorway. Adele thought she heard the sound of approaching footsteps.

But they were coming too slowly. The urgency wasn't being communicated.

She reached up with her, trying to gouge at the killer's face. He still had one of her fingers gripped. He was doing everything he could to crack it.

"Get off," he emitted in a wild, uncontrolled yodel of a scream, "you can't keep us apart!"

Adele was forced to retreat, to save her hand. She stumbled off the woman, twisting again, pirouetting clumsily, and using the momentum of the killer's attack to stumble back towards the toppled dresser.

For a brief moment, she stood facing the bed, panting heavily. The woman's face was still discolored. She wasn't breathing. Her chest wasn't moving. Adele didn't have the time for this.

"Get on the ground!" she shouted, reaching for her gun. But she couldn't risk hitting the woman.

And of course, he didn't comply. He didn't go back towards the woman, though, either. He stared at Adele, as if he had seen a ghost.

His eyes flitted from her face to the woman on the bed, then back up again.

"Devana?" he said in a hoarse tone. He reached up delicately with the same hand he had just tried to use to break her fingers and wiped away a tear.

And then he smiled. The largest, most joyful, beaming grin sprouted across his face.

"Devana," he exclaimed in delight. Like a child on Christmas morning, he stared at her in awe.

He glanced back at the prostitute on the bed and his expression flickered again into a frown. He looked at Adele, back to the prostitute, confused.

And then Adele realized, in the killer's delusional state, he thought he was seeing double. Athletic, blonde, tall, attractive according to some, and European. Adele checked all the boxes.

The executive had warned her. But in that moment, the similarities in their appearances were saving the strangled woman's life. She couldn't breathe. But for the moment he wasn't throttling her further. Still, Adele knew she only had seconds before the woman's brain was too deprived of oxygen to ever come back. She needed to administer CPR, and she couldn't wait. There was no time.

The killer crouched on the bed, blinking in confusion and staring from his prey to the DGSI agent. Adele still didn't have a clear shot. She swallowed and tried a more cautious approach this time.

She held out a hand, slowly, "Hello," she said, "It's me. Devana. It's good to see you...er, again?" She tried not to phrase it as too much of a question. Plausible deniability.

He chuckled, patting the bed. "Come in. Come in. I've been waiting for you."

Again, his expression flickered as he spotted the strangled woman on his bed. She wasn't sure what was happening in that splintered mind of his, but he was clearly struggling to make sense.

"I'll just come closer then, shall I?" Adele said, taking another step forward. She needed to subdue him, quickly. Needed to administer CPR.

"Of course. You know you're always welcome. You've always been welcome." He beamed. He pursed his lips, leaning in, his eyes fluttering behind those glasses.

Was he trying to get a kiss?

Adele felt shivers. But she took another step forward. She glanced towards the woman. Adele's fingers grazed the woman's arm. Her skin felt cold. Hopefully that was just Adele's imagination. The man was still pursing his lips, his eyes fluttering as he awaited her lips to lock with his. Whatever delusional land he was vacationing in, Adele wanted no part of it. So she *thwacked* him a good one. Right to the throat with her thumb.

He gurgled, gasping, doubling over.

Adele tried to bring her knee up into his face.

But again, he was faster than she had first anticipated. He howled, but the sound was half strangled from his choking. He did, however, manage to wrap his arms around her. He took her away from the bed, sending both of them sprawling.

Adele hit the ground, wondering where in the hell security was.

She could still hear footsteps, shouting. The voices.

Would no one come and help?

The man was on top of her now. He was still choking, spluttering. He tried to speak, but his voice came out hoarse, and spittle flecked her cheeks. He was crying again. But now, she could see the purple tint of rage bulging in his veins. His hands reached down, grasping at her neck and squeezing desperately.

"You never loved me," he finally rasped out. "I understand now. You never loved me."

If Adele could've nodded, she would have. But for the moment she was busy trying not to suffocate. She twisted, shifting. But he was strong. Way stronger than he looked. His hands continued to choke. She could feel herself going lightheaded. Her neck ached. Dark spots moved across her eyes.

She bent at his fingers, prying one free. She managed to take a sucking breath, but it wasn't much. Her lungs protested; her throat pulsed. She tried to twist her head, to turn away. But giving him her back would only cause more trouble.

He managed to tear his hands from her grip. Again, he doubled down on the pressure, leaning hard against her neck.

She shifted again. Instead of trying to move his hands from her throat, she moved her legs.

Aimed. And then swung her knee up as hard as she could.

It seemed fitting, in a place like this, where such an apparatus caused so much pleasure, the same center of male gravity would be his downfall. Her knee caught him right in the crown jewels.

He let out a squeak like a deflating balloon. She kicked again, with just as much force. No mercy.

His eyes bulged, he toppled off her. But again, displaying more fight than a man like him looked to possess, he grabbed at her, jerking at her wrist. Her bad shoulder pulsed in pain. She tried to yank free, but even wheezing, whining in pain, he held on as if she were some lifeline.

"Please!" he screamed, groaning, spittle flying. "Don't leave me again!"

She tried to pull free, but he kept a tight grip, still doubled over, bent on the ground, but his fingers like a vice. Like a terrified child holding onto their mother before the first day of school. The desperation was communicated in every twitch of a finger, every moan from his lips.

But he was holding her back from helping Devana.

A part of Adele was tempted to pity. But another part of her knew she couldn't hesitate.

She bent at the man's fingers, ripping them free and flinging him off her. Now he just rolled on the ground in pain, sobbing, clutching his crotch.

Adele nearly tripped over his swishing feet, but managed to remain upright, stumbling towards the bed.

The killer wheezed, and she didn't have time to contain him.

Adele nearly tripped over him again as she lunged towards Devana, gasping herself. Adele massaged her throat but didn't have time to check and see if any permanent damage had been done.

With a lurching step, she reached the victim on the bed.

"Adele!" a voice shouted.

A familiar, welcome voice. Adele tried to call out, but her throat hurt too much. He'd only been a few minutes behind her. Back-up had finally arrived. She tried again to call out. "John!" she said, her voice like that of a smoker. He wouldn't be able to hear her.

Fortunately, Agent Renee was able to follow the commotion. The big man emerged in the door. He took one look at the scene, cursed, and bounded over the dresser in a single leap. He landed next to the killer, shouting, "Adele! Are you okay? Paramedics are en route!"

Adele rasped, "Too late for paramedics. Contain him. I've got this."

John nodded, frantically glancing at her and the woman on the bed. The man on the ground was rolling about, clutching his testicles.

John put his knee in the man's back, holding him still. A flash of silver as Renee went for his cuffs.

But that was all Adele saw. Chest compressions. More chest compressions.

She hummed the rhythm in her head, following the beat, as she tried to resuscitate Devana.

"Come on," Adele whispered. "Come on!"

Fingers pressed against each other, quick, pulsating motions against the sternum. Faster, faster.

"Come on," Adele yelled in the face of the strangled woman.

John had cuffed the man behind her.

Everything seemed to have gone silent. Even the chattering voices and the motion from out in the hall went quiet.

The woman wasn't breathing. She wasn't moving. But Adele refused to give up.

Again. She pressed. Again.

"Adele," John said, in a slow, grim voice.

"Come on," Adele said, louder.

More chest compressions.

Adele's fingers were beginning to hurt. Her own eyes started to prickle. Adele's neck also felt on fire.

"Adele," John murmured, his hand touching her shoulder.

But again, Adele kept going.

Again.

The paramedics were too far. She'd come so quickly. She'd come as fast as she could. She couldn't let this woman die. She couldn't. In a strange way, Adele didn't just look like Devana. Devana looked like Adele.

Yet their lives were so very different.

Adele tried not to think too much about the last person she could've saved from suffocating. At that time, he had drowned. No air to his lungs either.

Not again. Not this time.

Could she ever have done this with her mother's killer? Tried to save his life? Tried to resuscitate him?

As she continued, she realized there wasn't a chance in hell she would've saved the man who'd killed half the people she ever loved. Not like this. There was something intimate about the nearness of it. The quick motions against the chest. And then finally, Adele gave the last, straining push of her hands against the woman's sternum...

And...

Devana coughed. Her eyes fluttered, and she let out a long, eerie groan. The mewl of a resurrected body. The groan of someone who had seen the other side of death.

Adele's heart pounded.

"She's alive! Holy shit. She's alive—Devana! Can you hear me?"

Agent Renee was muttering to himself in stunned awe. Adele saw him lift his phone. "Hurry," Renee was saying. "Send the paramedics in. We need them *now*."

Adele straightened up, breathing heavily, her fingers buzzing, her arms aching. Her shoulder throbbed in pain. Her neck was still tense.

Devana coughed again, staring at the ceiling, and breathing slowly, in faint, wheezing puffs.

Adele felt tears in her eyes.

In the distance, the sound of sirens was rapidly approaching.

Adele just stared at Devana. She'd gotten here in time. She'd done it. They'd saved her. Adele didn't even spare another glance towards the man on the floor.

There was something very forgettable about him.

CHAPTER THIRTY

She glanced at her phone. Three calls now, straight to voicemail. Her father wasn't picking up. She didn't even know if he had managed to get home.

She placed her phone in her pocket, resisting the urge to just turn it off.

Adele sat beneath the moon on the hood of her car outside the police station. In the depths of night, the parking lot had dwindled. Shadows moved across the illuminated glass doors of the precinct behind her.

Adele rubbed at her sore shoulder, feeling the way her muscles went taut.

She let out a faint sigh, glancing up at the moon. There was something almost peaceful about sitting there, alone, in the dark, under a celestial spotlight.

But it was a melancholy peace.

Silence had its own sort of pain.

She heard the swish of the sliding doors behind her. The sound of footsteps, boots against gravel. And then the car dipped as a large form settled on the hood next to her.

She glanced over at Agent Renee. "You're going to dent the thing," she muttered.

He snorted, and leaned in, resting his head on her shoulder.

"I'm tired, Adele. I need my beauty sleep."

She winced. He was reclining against her bad arm. But she didn't have the heart to tell him. Besides, despite the pain, there was something comforting about having Renee there with her.

"Good job back there," she said, resting her head against his own bowed form.

She wasn't sure what the executive would think if he could see them now. It was a bit uncomfortable to treat John like anything other than a coworker within line of sight of a police station. Granted, a foreign police station.

But she was just too weary to care. Besides, things often went overlooked in the dead of night.

"I didn't do anything," John said. "That was all you. I think you kicked him so hard he lost some of his grandkids."

"I'm not sure he's going to have that option where he's going."

John nodded, his hair bristling against her cheek.

"My dad's not calling back," she murmured.

John sat up, glancing at her. "You never did say why he left so quickly."

"I told him."

"Told him? Wait. *Told him*?"

Adele nodded.

John ran a hand across his chin. "Shit."

"Exactly."

They both exhaled at the same time, twin sighs meandering on the night.

"How did he take it?"

"About as well as can be expected."

John winced, leaning back. "That bad? I'm sorry."

Adele shook her head. "You're teasing?"

John considered the question. Then he nodded. "A little. Your dad's a strange one; but I am sorry."

She leaned against him more fully. Damn the cops behind them. Damn the executive. She didn't care what any of them thought. John was the only one who accepted her for who she was. For what she had done. She didn't think of herself as the worst thing she had ever done. And neither did John. That was the point. He made space for her failure. Why couldn't her father be like that? As she thought it, she felt a bolt of rage. A sudden surge of absolute anger. She scowled, bunching her fists in her lap.

"What are you thinking?" John said in a sleepy voice.

"My childhood was stolen."

"If you find yours, see if mine is there with it."

Adele shook her head. "I'm serious. My dad was never a very affectionate man. I thought things were mending between us. I was hoping they were. I thought maybe I could have a father. You know, later in life. John," she said, her voice shaking, "when I was in that park, watching him drown, part of me almost thought my dad would thank me. Maybe even love me for it. We had both wanted him caught for nearly a decade. I did what he always wanted. Why isn't he returning my calls?"

John's long arm reached around her, embracing her and pulling her close.

"Thick skulls sometimes take a bit longer. Trust me. Personal experience."

Adele gave a little chuckle, hidden in a sob. She shook her head, closing her eyes. "I still don't think I did the right thing back there."

John grunted. "Maybe not. Maybe. But you did it. You can't change that, Adele. You're not perfect. I know you try to be. But you're human, just like the rest of us." He gave her a quick squeeze. "Some of just have a bit more fun with our humanity."

Adele felt a lump in her throat. To deflect, she forced a chuckle and said, "My dad still pretends like he doesn't know your name."

"And I pretend like he doesn't smell like mushrooms. It's a give and take relationship."

Adele snorted with laughter. John joined her a second later. They were both so very tired. And yet it was nice to just sit out there, laughing at jokes that weren't too funny, in the dark, like a couple of high school kids again. Adele thought of a previous life, a more innocent one. She missed it. And she was so very tired of this one. But with John, it wasn't so bad.

"Flight leaves early tomorrow," John said. "We should get some sleep."

"Are you coming on to me?"

John leaned in, kissing her on the cheek. "Always. I'll drive. But really, we need to sleep. I don't want to have to give a report with bedhead."

Adele smirked at the mental image and slowly pushed off the hood of the car. John got off as well, and the vehicle almost gave a creak of gratitude.

The two agents circled the vehicle, moving into the car, and shutting themselves off from the night.

EPILOGUE

Adele let out a long sigh of relief as she pushed through the front door to her apartment complex. She hefted her briefcase and her small piece of carry-on luggage. Her arm was tired. Her feet were tired. She was tired. Morning sunlight streamed through the glass behind her as she slowly trudged up the steps that led to her unit.

John had slept the entire plane ride from Germany. The taxi had dropped her off first, and now she shot a glance over her shoulder, barely moving. Through the crescent window above the door, she watched as the taxi, still carrying Agent Renee, dwindled into the distance, turning up the main road.

She turned back to the stairs. Almost home. And then she would sleep.

No. Pistachio ice cream. *Then* sleep.

She allowed a faint smile. Her father still wasn't returning her calls. But she was going to listen to John. Give it a few days. Maybe a couple of weeks.

Besides, her relationship with Renee was the closest one she'd ever had with a man.

He had even invited her for dinner tonight, with his daughter.

Pistachio ice cream. Sleep. More ice cream. Another nap. Then dinner with Renee and his progeny. It was going to be a good day.

She reached the top of the stairs and took the next set until she reached the third floor.

Her steps were slow, lethargic. Her mind was spent. This last case had been a draining one. But at least it had ended with a saved life. Still, so many others had died. Sometimes, Adele felt guilty when she took days off. How many killers were out there, at that very moment? How many victims was she not there for? How many people were just now breathing their last, while she dreamt of ice cream.

Her stomach twisted as if someone had jammed a knife between her ribs.

She knew she couldn't think like that. She had to rest. Had to pace herself. If she killed herself from overwork, she would be robbing potential victims for the next forty years of someone who could take their cause.

At least, that's what she had to tell herself. And she believed it. Partly.

Her mind was spinning, though, from lack of sleep. The hotel bed had been lumpy.

She marched to her door, fishing out her keys. She unlocked and pulled the door open slowly, rolling her shoulders as she did. The small piece of tape she had taken to sticking just near the bottom hinge was still there.

She supposed she wouldn't have to take those precautions anymore. With the painter dead, she was safe. She smiled at the thought of safety. Rest. She bent over, pulling at the tape, and tearing it off.

If anyone came through, the tape would rip the small string looped around the edge of the door, and she would know someone had been in her place.

She pushed into the apartment, lowering her bags to the floor.

She kicked the door shut behind her with her heel, rubbing at the back of her neck.

The space smelled clean. She hadn't completely washed the dishes before leaving a few days ago. But at least she had rinsed them, so it hadn't stunk up the place.

She began moving for the freezer, envisioning that big two-gallon tub of pistachio goodness she had purchased just the previous week. A small, guilty part of her didn't want to see how much was already gone.

As she approached the freezer, she could feel stress, exhaustion melting from her shoulders. The cape of darkness that had come with the De Wallen night also seemed to lift. There was just something so... comforting about home. A part of her felt a jolt of sadness as she remembered something Robert Henry had said.

She hadn't thought she'd grown up with a home, moving so much. But he'd told her perhaps she just was lucky enough to have more than one.

Was that how the Belgian prostitutes had felt? Leaving their countries due to legal troubles or to find safer work?

Or had they died far from their homes, alone?

Adele gave herself a moment to remember why it was she did this job anyway. People deserved to live to see their homes. People deserved better... Or maybe deserve didn't have anything to do with it.

Adele just wanted to give them better.

As she considered this, feeling a strange welling of emotion following her multiple nights of poor sleep, she glanced around the kitchen and then went still. Her brow twitched into a frown.

She wasn't sure what caught her attention at first. Her mind was used to picking out details. She was trained to focus on the small things.

And now, staring, she realized what it was.

The dishes were in the wrong sink.

There were two sinks. One faucet. She put her dishes on the left. That was for dirty.

Why were they now on the right?

Not only that, but there was no silverware with the dishes.

Her nose twitched, and she reached up to scratch it.

She just stared perplexed. Had John been—no, he'd been with her.

Her father? No. He didn't have a key. The taped string was still on the door.

Was she just remembering things wrong?

She'd had a piece of chicken parmesan. She'd used a steak knife, but the knife was missing. The fork was there, just visible beneath the plates.

She leaned in, tilting the dishes but it wasn't there. Why were the dishes in the wrong sink? And where was the steak knife?

Adele's mind was still trying to catch up with the silliness of it all.

She was seeing ghosts where there were none. Sometimes, after a case, it could take a few days to reset.

She swallowed faintly. She was just being silly. That was all. Silly. The painter was still haunting her... But she'd won. She'd beat him.

She forced a little smile, chuckling. She moved the dishes into the proper sink, turning on the water to rinse them.

There was no knife. It wasn't on the counter.

Sometimes, she just wished her mind would let things go.

But other times, a slow, prickling sense of realization would dawn on her, moments before something clicked.

The pieces fell into place quickly. Someone had been in her apartment. They had moved the dishes and taken the knife. The painter was dead. John and her father had been in Germany with her. The tape was still on the door. Whoever had been here had come through a window or had known to check for markers by the hinges.

In the case of this second option, whoever had been here was dangerous. Law enforcement?

Adele spine prickled. She immediately pictured Agent Paige.

What if she was under investigation? What if they knew about the painter?

Adele bit her lip. She glanced around the room, desperately

searching for any sign of new plaster hiding a wire.

She'd installed some of her own in the past. She knew where to look.

And yet even as her mind spun, trying to make sense, her gaze moved back towards the sink.

Someone trained had come into her apartment. Why in the hell would they take a steak knife? If she was under investigation, Paige wouldn't burgle cutlery.

All of this processed rapidly through Adele's mind. Quick, pulsing strands of thought, tying together to try and paint a picture. But it didn't make sense. The pieces didn't fit. She was missing information.

It was like this, standing in her own kitchen, facing the sink, that she felt the sudden lance of pain in her ribs.

She winced and glanced down. "Oh," she said faintly, staring at the steak knife jammed between her ribs.

It all felt so surreal. Adele just stared as blood began to spill down her stomach. She blinked. A second later, a shockwave of agony hit her.

She let out a painful hiss.

And that's when she saw the man.

He must've been hiding down the hall in one of the rooms. He had moved so quietly she hadn't heard a thing.

A man wearing a dark ski mask, standing behind her, one hand extended where he had jammed the knife into her. He had moved so damn quietly. He had known to check the hinges. He had snuck into her apartment.

Along with the pain, before the inevitable surge of action, Adele felt a flicker of fear. She didn't have a clue who this was.

And then all hell broke loose.

Adele yelled, bleeding, in pain, but grabbed one of the dishes from the sink and swung it as hard as she could.

The man behind her moved fast. He ducked the swing. But as he moved, he suddenly grunted in pain. His motions were those of a young man but his sudden freezing, and gasp, was an older one. Or an injured one. His body didn't bend how it should have, and her plate smashed into his face.

The thing shattered. The man in the ski mask tumbled back.

"Get the hell out!" she screamed. Mostly just to make a sound, to jar the man with shock at the noise. And to hopefully alert the neighbors.

She grabbed another plate.

The man was stumbling, reaching up and dislodging pieces from his mask. Blood came away on his hand. A gloved hand—the red slick against brown leather.

Adele flung this next plate, and a second later realized she was still wearing her weapon.

The man's eyes darted to her hip at the same time as her hand went for her gun.

Reeling, bloody, he cursed, spun on his heel, and sprinted towards the door.

Adele yanked her weapon from her holster.

But he was so very fast. And she was slow. *Far* slower than she should have been.

The man sprinted out of her apartment, leaving the door open as he raced away.

Adele's hand gripping her weapon trembled, and then went limp. The gun fell, clattering to the floor.

Only then did Adele realize blood was pooling down her hip along her leg and puddling onto the floor by her shoe.

"Oh, right. The knife," Adele murmured, as if she were commenting on the weather.

The shock hit her now. The pain was coming in waves. Her knees buckled, and Adele let out a faint little gasp.

She hoped this wouldn't make her late for dinner with John.

She wasn't thinking straight. Her phone. She should call for someone.

The blood kept pooling.

The same hand that had dropped the gun felt paralyzed. She couldn't reach for her phone. Her body was shutting down. Her eyes were blinking but failing to see as dark spots swallowed her vision.

She couldn't see. Even the pain was diminishing.

That was nice. She mumbled something. Something incoherent. She was really looking forward to dinner.

Blood continued to spread, the knife buried between her ribs. Then all thought faded completely.

NOW AVAILABLE!

LEFT TO HARM
(An Adele Sharp Mystery—Book 15)

The #1 bestselling series! In a busy train station in Europe, a tourist finds a finger in a train station locker—and soon after, a matching body is discovered on the train. A new serial killer is at work, more cunning and diabolical than anyone can imagine—and FBI Special Agent is the only one who can stop him before he strikes again.

"When you think that life cannot get better, Blake Pierce comes up with another masterpiece of thriller and mystery! This book is full of twists and the end brings a surprising revelation. I strongly recommend this book to the permanent library of any reader that enjoys a very well written thriller."
--Books and Movie Reviews, Roberto Mattos (re Almost Gone)

LEFT TO HARM is book #15 in the #1 bestselling FBI thriller series featuring Adele Sharp (the series begins with LEFT TO DIE, book #1) by USA Today bestselling author Blake Pierce, whose #1 bestseller Once Gone (a free download) has received over 1,000 five-star reviews.

FBI special agent Adele Sharp—a German-and-French raised American with triple citizenship—is made to criss-cross America and Europe to bring criminals to justice. But as more bodies begin to turn up, each missing a finger and abandoned on a train, Adele must race to uncover the meaning behind this twisted signature.

Can she enter the killer's mind in time to save the next victim?

Or will this case take a darker turn than even Adele could imagine?

An action-packed mystery series of international intrigue and riveting suspense, LEFT TO LOATHE will leave you turning pages late into the night.

Future books in the series will be available soon.

Blake Pierce

Blake Pierce is the USA Today bestselling author of the RILEY PAGE mystery series, which includes seventeen books. Blake Pierce is also the author of the MACKENZIE WHITE mystery series, comprising fourteen books; of the AVERY BLACK mystery series, comprising six books; of the KERI LOCKE mystery series, comprising five books; of the MAKING OF RILEY PAIGE mystery series, comprising six books; of the KATE WISE mystery series, comprising seven books; of the CHLOE FINE psychological suspense mystery, comprising six books; of the JESSE HUNT psychological suspense thriller series, comprising twenty four books; of the AU PAIR psychological suspense thriller series, comprising three books; of the ZOE PRIME mystery series, comprising six books; of the ADELE SHARP mystery series, comprising fifteen books, of the EUROPEAN VOYAGE cozy mystery series, comprising four books; of the new LAURA FROST FBI suspense thriller, comprising nine books (and counting); of the new ELLA DARK FBI suspense thriller, comprising eleven books (and counting); of the A YEAR IN EUROPE cozy mystery series, comprising nine books, of the AVA GOLD mystery series, comprising six books (and counting); of the RACHEL GIFT mystery series, comprising six books (and counting); of the VALERIE LAW mystery series, comprising six books (and counting); of the PAIGE KING mystery series, comprising six books (and counting); and of the MAY MOORE mystery series, comprising three books (and counting).

An avid reader and lifelong fan of the mystery and thriller genres, Blake loves to hear from you, so please feel free to visit www.blakepierceauthor.com to learn more and stay in touch.

BOOKS BY BLAKE PIERCE

MAY MOORE MYSTERY SERIES
NEVER RUN (Book #1)
NEVER TELL (Book #2)
NEVER LIVE (Book #3)

PAIGE KING MYSTERY SERIES
THE GIRL HE PINED (Book #1)
THE GIRL HE CHOSE (Book #2)
THE GIRL HE TOOK (Book #3)
THE GIRL HE WISHED (Book #4)
THE GIRL HE CROWNED (Book #5)
THE GIRL HE WATCHED (Book #6)

VALERIE LAW MYSTERY SERIES
NO MERCY (Book #1)
NO PITY (Book #2)
NO FEAR (Book #3)
NO SLEEP (Book #4)
NO QUARTER (Book #5)
NO CHANCE (Book #6)

RACHEL GIFT MYSTERY SERIES
HER LAST WISH (Book #1)
HER LAST CHANCE (Book #2)
HER LAST HOPE (Book #3)
HER LAST FEAR (Book #4)
HER LAST CHOICE (Book #5)
HER LAST BREATH (Book #6)

AVA GOLD MYSTERY SERIES
CITY OF PREY (Book #1)
CITY OF FEAR (Book #2)
CITY OF BONES (Book #3)
CITY OF GHOSTS (Book #4)
CITY OF DEATH (Book #5)
CITY OF VICE (Book #6)

A YEAR IN EUROPE
A MURDER IN PARIS (Book #1)
DEATH IN FLORENCE (Book #2)
VENGEANCE IN VIENNA (Book #3)
A FATALITY IN SPAIN (Book #4)

ELLA DARK FBI SUSPENSE THRILLER
GIRL, ALONE (Book #1)
GIRL, TAKEN (Book #2)
GIRL, HUNTED (Book #3)
GIRL, SILENCED (Book #4)
GIRL, VANISHED (Book 5)
GIRL ERASED (Book #6)
GIRL, FORSAKEN (Book #7)
GIRL, TRAPPED (Book #8)
GIRL, EXPENDABLE (Book #9)
GIRL, ESCAPED (Book #10)
GIRL, HIS (Book #11)

LAURA FROST FBI SUSPENSE THRILLER
ALREADY GONE (Book #1)
ALREADY SEEN (Book #2)
ALREADY TRAPPED (Book #3)
ALREADY MISSING (Book #4)
ALREADY DEAD (Book #5)
ALREADY TAKEN (Book #6)
ALREADY CHOSEN (Book #7)
ALREADY LOST (Book #8)
ALREADY HIS (Book #9)

EUROPEAN VOYAGE COZY MYSTERY SERIES
MURDER (AND BAKLAVA) (Book #1)
DEATH (AND APPLE STRUDEL) (Book #2)
CRIME (AND LAGER) (Book #3)
MISFORTUNE (AND GOUDA) (Book #4)
CALAMITY (AND A DANISH) (Book #5)
MAYHEM (AND HERRING) (Book #6)

ADELE SHARP MYSTERY SERIES
LEFT TO DIE (Book #1)

LEFT TO RUN (Book #2)
LEFT TO HIDE (Book #3)
LEFT TO KILL (Book #4)
LEFT TO MURDER (Book #5)
LEFT TO ENVY (Book #6)
LEFT TO LAPSE (Book #7)
LEFT TO VANISH (Book #8)
LEFT TO HUNT (Book #9)
LEFT TO FEAR (Book #10)
LEFT TO PREY (Book #11)
LEFT TO LURE (Book #12)
LEFT TO CRAVE (Book #13)
LEFT TO LOATHE (Book #14)
LEFT TO HARM (Book #15)

THE AU PAIR SERIES
ALMOST GONE (Book#1)
ALMOST LOST (Book #2)
ALMOST DEAD (Book #3)

ZOE PRIME MYSTERY SERIES
FACE OF DEATH (Book#1)
FACE OF MURDER (Book #2)
FACE OF FEAR (Book #3)
FACE OF MADNESS (Book #4)
FACE OF FURY (Book #5)
FACE OF DARKNESS (Book #6)

A JESSIE HUNT PSYCHOLOGICAL SUSPENSE SERIES
THE PERFECT WIFE (Book #1)
THE PERFECT BLOCK (Book #2)
THE PERFECT HOUSE (Book #3)
THE PERFECT SMILE (Book #4)
THE PERFECT LIE (Book #5)
THE PERFECT LOOK (Book #6)
THE PERFECT AFFAIR (Book #7)
THE PERFECT ALIBI (Book #8)
THE PERFECT NEIGHBOR (Book #9)
THE PERFECT DISGUISE (Book #10)
THE PERFECT SECRET (Book #11)
THE PERFECT FAÇADE (Book #12)

THE PERFECT IMPRESSION (Book #13)
THE PERFECT DECEIT (Book #14)
THE PERFECT MISTRESS (Book #15)
THE PERFECT IMAGE (Book #16)
THE PERFECT VEIL (Book #17)
THE PERFECT INDISCRETION (Book #18)
THE PERFECT RUMOR (Book #19)
THE PERFECT COUPLE (Book #20)
THE PERFECT MURDER (Book #21)
THE PERFECT HUSBAND (Book #22)
THE PERFECT SCANDAL (Book #23)
THE PERFECT MASK (Book #24)

CHLOE FINE PSYCHOLOGICAL SUSPENSE SERIES
NEXT DOOR (Book #1)
A NEIGHBOR'S LIE (Book #2)
CUL DE SAC (Book #3)
SILENT NEIGHBOR (Book #4)
HOMECOMING (Book #5)
TINTED WINDOWS (Book #6)

KATE WISE MYSTERY SERIES
IF SHE KNEW (Book #1)
IF SHE SAW (Book #2)
IF SHE RAN (Book #3)
IF SHE HID (Book #4)
IF SHE FLED (Book #5)
IF SHE FEARED (Book #6)
IF SHE HEARD (Book #7)

THE MAKING OF RILEY PAIGE SERIES
WATCHING (Book #1)
WAITING (Book #2)
LURING (Book #3)
TAKING (Book #4)
STALKING (Book #5)
KILLING (Book #6)

RILEY PAIGE MYSTERY SERIES
ONCE GONE (Book #1)

ONCE TAKEN (Book #2)
ONCE CRAVED (Book #3)
ONCE LURED (Book #4)
ONCE HUNTED (Book #5)
ONCE PINED (Book #6)
ONCE FORSAKEN (Book #7)
ONCE COLD (Book #8)
ONCE STALKED (Book #9)
ONCE LOST (Book #10)
ONCE BURIED (Book #11)
ONCE BOUND (Book #12)
ONCE TRAPPED (Book #13)
ONCE DORMANT (Book #14)
ONCE SHUNNED (Book #15)
ONCE MISSED (Book #16)
ONCE CHOSEN (Book #17)

MACKENZIE WHITE MYSTERY SERIES
BEFORE HE KILLS (Book #1)
BEFORE HE SEES (Book #2)
BEFORE HE COVETS (Book #3)
BEFORE HE TAKES (Book #4)
BEFORE HE NEEDS (Book #5)
BEFORE HE FEELS (Book #6)
BEFORE HE SINS (Book #7)
BEFORE HE HUNTS (Book #8)
BEFORE HE PREYS (Book #9)
BEFORE HE LONGS (Book #10)
BEFORE HE LAPSES (Book #11)
BEFORE HE ENVIES (Book #12)
BEFORE HE STALKS (Book #13)
BEFORE HE HARMS (Book #14)

AVERY BLACK MYSTERY SERIES
CAUSE TO KILL (Book #1)
CAUSE TO RUN (Book #2)
CAUSE TO HIDE (Book #3)
CAUSE TO FEAR (Book #4)
CAUSE TO SAVE (Book #5)
CAUSE TO DREAD (Book #6)

www.ingramcontent.com/pod-product-compliance
Lightning Source LLC
Chambersburg PA
CBHW021659110726
47902CB00007B/1995